Son of Fire

LARRY L. KING

PublishAmerica
Baltimore

Softcover 9781627092111
PUBLISHED BY PUBLISHAMERICA, LLLP
www.publishamerica.com
Baltimore

Printed in the United States of America

DEDICATION

July 1997 during a Monday night visitation program from my church, a fellow deacon and I rang the doorbell at Wanda Eckman's home. She had been widowed nineteen months before, as was I eight months ago. She made quite an impression on me and I was unable to get her out of my mind, not that I wanted too. After several attempts to call her and each time losing my nerve, I finally left a message on her answering machine. Later that night she returned my call. After several minutes of beating around the bush, I asked her if she would have dinner with me. I was just a little rusty asking for a date, but she said yes and we started dating in August. I knew from the start that she was special and I wanted our relationship to go on forever.

We were married January 10, 1998 and I must say she has been a great motivator for me. I started making up and telling her bedtime stories while we were lying in bed. The subject matter varied from night to night, but never 'X' rated. She said she enjoyed my stories, I hope she did because it encouraged me to put some of these thoughts on paper. I asked her to perform the task of proofreading my stories. That is not an easy task, because my thoughts often outrun my slow typing fingers. Words would be left out and very confusing at times. Wanda is always the proto-type for the women in my stories. The men in my stories are head over heels in love with their ladies, as I am with her. Without her help and support, none of my stories would be complete or completed. Thanks, Wanda. I love you more than the words of a mere mortal man can express.

—*Larry*

FORWARD

My father's mother was one quarter Cherokee. We called her Mamma Nell. This is her family's story covering about one hundred years, beginning with my great-great-great grandfather, Robert Henry 'Bob' Mace and his wife Rose. Bob and Rose were full-blood Cherokee living. My story will continue with their son Benjamin 'Ben' Mace and his first wife Susannah. She was a beautiful, but fragile, English girl. She was unable to bear children and died at very young age. After a period of mourning, Ben married Betsy and later a son was born. This son, Don Pedro Mace was my grandmother's father. The Mace family was Cherokee and lived in North Carolina in the early 1800's. They migrated from North Carolina to Arkansas and later to Texas after the Civil War. Why did they leave their North Carolina home? I can only speculate, perhaps they were involved in the forced relocation of the Cherokee people from Tennessee to western Oklahoma during the winter of 1838-1839 that became known as the 'Trail Of Tears', Although some of the events recorded in this story are historical, the stories of the Mace family and their friendship with Chief John Ross are fiction. Interwoven into the story is the similar story of the King family as they also migrated from North Carolina (about a hundred mile from the Mace family) to Red River County, Texas

Larry L. King, Sr.

CONTENTS

EARLY LIFE

The Europeans

There is an old Cherokee saying, "We will be remembered by the tracks that we leave". These are the tracks of *'Ooh Way Chee Ah Chee La'* which means Son of Fire. I want to tell you his story, my great-great-great grandfather.

An old man was down by the sea early in the morning taking his daily stroll and his time of meditation. He stopped and sat down on a rock. This had been his place of meditation since he was a young man. On this day his grandson had followed him and was in the woods a few feet behind the rock his grandfather was on. Something on the water caught the eye of both the old man and his grandson. The silence was broken by the young boy.

"Paw-Paw, what is that?" the boy shouts and startles the old man.

The old man jumps and replies, "I don't know! Come here and watch with me".

The boy joins his grandfather on the rock and they continue looking at the object far on the horizon. After watching this thing getting larger and larger with the passing of many hours, they realize the object is nothing like they have ever seen before. As it came closer, the old man says, "It looks like a large boat with three trees with giant white bulging leaves. I've never seen anything larger than a canoe. Let's go into town and get a closer look at this thing."

The year was 1635 near Boston. Tall ships had been in and out of this harbor many times before, but this was the first time the old man had seen one. Being an American Indian this was all new to him. The date was the eight day of October. The old man began asking questions of the people as they came off the ship.

He asked a man in uniform on the dock, "What is this thing and where did it come from"?

"My name is Robert Hackwell. I am the commander of this ship. It is The Abigail of London. We departed Plymouth England on June 4, 1635. --- Please try to stay out of the way!"

The old man and his grandson moved on down the dock a little and encountered a younger man and asked him for more information. "What is your name?"

"William King." He replied. "You really should be here. --- We've been on the water for a long time and our journey was not without hardships. Many on board came down with smallpox. I've been treating the sick even though I've had no formal medical training and for some reason I didn't contract the disease. Most of the people recovered, but death took about a third of the cases. --- If you stay here you and the boy may get sick. Please for your sake, move away from this area as quickly as you can!"

The old man took his advice and left the dock area. William King was a young Irish lad of 28 years. This was his arrival to the new world.

One hundred sixty eight years later descendants of the old man brought forth a child. The child's Cherokee name was Son of Fire and Christian name Robert Henry Mace. This is my great-great-great grandfather and this is his story and the tracks he left.

His life began in what is present day North Carolina.

Although the Cherokee had been hunters and lived off what the land provided for centuries, they adopted the European's life style of farming. Over time Robert's family became farmers as they struggled to cling to the traditions of their ancestors.

When Robert was 9 years old there was to be a tribal meeting in Echota in what is now Tennessee in the spring. In the evening on the eve of that day Robert's father asked, "My son, would you like to attend this year's tribal council with me?"

His father was a member of the seventeen member council and he was eager for his son to become involved with tribal affairs. The events of that meeting would change the destiny of the young boy.

"Yes, papa!" came the words of a very excited young boy, scarcely before the words had escaped his father's mouth. Bob, as his family called him, had dreamed of this day for a long time. Bob was eager to become a man and make his place in the tribe.

"Good, Bob! I know you're only 9, but you will soon be a man and I want you to be active in the tribe's affairs. We will leave at first light on the morrow." His father replied.

Bob was pleased his father thought of him as soon becoming a man, but he was also happy to remain a child for now.

Bob's father was to give a speech before the vote for his re-election at the council meeting and yet neither father nor son knew the full impact of the meeting this year. The destiny of Bob and another boy at the meeting was set in motion.

Bob and his dad made good time on the first day of their journey. In the evening before sunset they made camp alongside a gentle stream. After starting a fire, they dined on jerky and corn from their pouch. Bob's father finished preparing his speech to be presented at the council meeting. The young boy's only thoughts were those of a normal 9-year old. His only thoughts were of adventure and give no thought to the future. As they retired for the evening, his dad reminded him that it was not possible for him to attend the actual council meetings, but Bob didn't mind. He had visions of the future when he would be addressing his son. As he lay beneath the stars with his head cradled in his hands cup behind his head, thoughts of the next day were quickly replaced with a deep sleep.

The song of the birds and the smell of burning oak from the campfire were his alarm as a new day was dawning. They only had a few more hours before reaching arriving at Echota. His father continued going over his speech, he wanted it to be perfect. When they reached Echota, Bob set about exploring the camp area and night came long before he wanted.

As the third day dawned and smell of the camp again signaled the beginning a wonderful day his father asked, "Bob, what are your plans for today?"

"Oh, I don't have a plan! Just see how many new friends I can meet today. Yesterday I noticed that there a few other boys here. I'm sure the day will go by very fast". He replied.

"Good, the meetings should last another day or two, but I should be finished early today. Don't get into trouble."

Bob knew his father was only kidding, but trouble had a way of finding him despite his good intentions. After his father left, he continued his survey of the camp. Bob was very outgoing and never met a stranger. As the day progressed he met quite a few boys his age in the camp and made new friends of them all. Then he met another boy that appeared to be a few years his senior, but he looked very strange to Bob. He immediately struck up a conversation with the older boy.

"What's your name?" Bob asked.

"My Cherokee name is *Guwisguwi*, but I'm called John Ross." He replied, "What's yours?"

"*Uwetsi Atsilv*, or Robert Henry Mace, but everyone calls me Bob. Why don't you have dark hair like me and skin like mine?"

John laughed, "You ask a lot of questions, but I hear that a lot. My father is from across the big water, a country called Scotland. That's where I get my red hair, but my mother is Cherokee and we live among her clan. We are from the Bird Clan. My father has become one of the important leaders in the tribe."

Bob was full of questions and asked again, "Where are you from?"

"I was born in Turkeytown near the Coosa River, but now we live in the Lookout Mountain area." John replied. "Where are you from?"

"Greensborough, that is about a 2 day journey east of here." Bob responded.

John seemed a little disappointed as he replied, "Oh... we are 3 days journey west of here. That's a long distance between us ... 5 day journey. I had hoped we lived closer to each other."

Bob was disappointed as well as he echoed John's, "That is a long distance!"

The two disappointed boys walked along the trail for awhile, kicking stones and throwing sticks at birds as they walked along dreaming of the future.

"How old are you?" John asked as he broke the silence.

"I'm 9, but everyone says I look much older?" Bob replied, "How old are you?"

"I'm 12 and yes, I would agree. I thought you were older." John responded.

"Do you like to hunt?" Bob asked.

"Oh … yes, just a few weeks ago I killed my first deer. My father was very proud and said the deer would provide food for our family for a long time. How about you … do you like to hunt?" John replied.

"Oh yes … and fish too. I got my first deer last year." Bob said.

The continued along the trail until they reached a pond where they sat to rest for a spell and gaze across the water.

Bob broke another short silence to issue a challenge to his new friend, "How many times can you skip a stone on the water?"

Bob had always enjoyed competition and wanted to see if his older companion was up to a little test of their abilities.

"Don't know … I never counted." John replied.

"My record is four times!" Bob said proudly. "Let's have a contest."

"A contest … what kind of contest?"

"Yes, let's see who can skip a stone the most times."

"What will the prize be?" John asked.

"Let me see, for a contest of this greatness the prize must be as grand. I know the winner will be the future chief of our people" Bob said.

"We are too lowly to ever become chief, but let's have the contest anyway." John said in a laughing tone.

Bob looked for a good flat stone and set it in flight across the water, counting as the stone skipped, "One, two, three ... see if you can beat that."

John selected a stone that in his mind was a winner and threw it across the water. "One, two, three, four ... I win!" John jumped up and down in a victory dance.

"Whoa, my friend, I must have a chance to equal your best. If I don't get four this time you are the winner."

Bob selected another stone and was successful in matching his new friend's mark. John likewise took another shot and skipped the stone five times. Bob had met his match; his next attempt came up short with only four skips.

"OK, you are the winner! From now on you will be 'Chief' to me."

During the remainder of the council meeting their friendship grew and the day they were to return home was a day of great sadness for them for the distance between them was great. It would be difficult to maintain their friendship with so many miles between them. However, their bond was strong as they made pledges to each other not to let this friendship wither away.

"Bob, we must write to each other until we meet again." John said.

"Yes, I would like that, 'Chief', I'll write as soon as I get home and tell you of our journey."

John also made the same pledge. The difference in their ages and the miles between them only strengthened their resolve to maintain their friendship. They exchanged letters often as the two grew into manhood. Over the years their friendship did not fade as had been their fear.

Bob developed a hunter's heart and the soul of a warrior and had wisdom far beyond his peers. Bob was from the AniWodi or Paint Clan. Members of his Clan made red paint for ceremonies and also provided most of the tribes Medicine Men. Adawehi or wise men also came from this clan. Bob's Cherokee name was *Uwetsi Atsilv*, which means Son of Fire. He developed into manhood fishing in Beaver Creek and roaming the forest hunting deer, wild boar and timber wolf. Bob spent weeks at a time in the wilderness with nothing but his rifle, hunting knife and a small hatchet that he carried in his belt in all of his wilderness wanderings. Bob now stood six feet tall and weighed 175 pounds. He was as strong as an ox and his muscles were as tight as a bowstring. All the young Indian maidens took notice of Bob because of his extreme good looks and his position among the tribe. Over the years he and his friend, John Ross, shared many business ventures and both were very successful. As well as being partners with John Ross, Bob had a very profitable farm and was considered a wealthy man, that didn't hurt either. He would be a good catch for any young maiden.

In the traditional Cherokee family the parents arranged for the marriages and it was traditional not to marry someone from your clan. Early in 1826 Bob met a young Indian maiden from the Blue Clan or AniSahomi, keepers of all children's medicines and caretakers of medicinal herb gardens. Her Cherokee name was *Tla-a-ta-di-u-s-ti Tsi* or Rose with No Thorns. Her English name was Telitha Bickle. Bob simply called her Rose. She was the loveliest maiden Bob had ever seen. Her hair was as black as a raven's wing, skin as smooth as a pond on still day and dark brown eyes that seemed to look deep inside his very soul. Bob was smitten by her looks, charm, and dignity from the start. And it was good that she was not from his clan. Everything was perfect for Bob and Rose to be married. Following Cherokee tradition a young man must ask for the hand of a maiden, but he must first prove that he can provide for his wife and take care of her. To do this he must first ask for her hand. If the "mothers" thought that this might be a good union, they gave a "tack approval" of the courtship. Then he must clear ground and plant a garden and erect a house for her to live in. This was to prove that he could provide for her and any children they may have. Once this has been proven, and this would take a full year, he would then again ask for her hand. If the mothers approved, then the wedding could proceed. The only thing the father did, openly, was to escort his daughter to the wedding circle.

As the day approached for the wedding, the holy man blessed the sacred spot for the ceremony for seven consecutive days and the ceremony followed.

On the day of the wedding Rose entered the sacred council fire area wearing a white dress and white moccasins, made from deerskins. Bob joined her wearing a traditional rose-colored ribbon shirt, black pants and moccasins. The holy man wrapped each of them in blue blankets, representing their old ways of weakness, sorrow, failures and spiritual depression. After they were wrapped in the blanket, their relatives followed them to the sacred fire.

The holy man blessed the union of Bob and Rose as well as

all those present. "Be shelter to each other so that neither feels the rain. Be warmth to each other so there is no cold. Although you are two people, only one life is before you. May your third companion be happiness and your days together be good and long. Now is the time to exchange gifts. Bob, what do you bring Rose?"

"Rose, I bring you this basket with meats and skins representing my promise to feed and clothe you."

"Rose, what do you bring to Bob?" The holy man asks.

"Bob, I bring you this basket with bread and corn representing my promise to nurture you."

The holy man instructs them, "Now, repeat the seven step vows around the fire."

Bob took the first step, stopped and repeated this vow:

> *Rose my beloved; our love has become firm by your walking one with me. Together we will share the responsibilities of the lodge, food and children. May the Creator bless noble children to share. May they live long.*

Rose took a step to join Bob and voiced her vow:

> *Bob, This is my commitment to you, my husband. Together we will share the responsibility of the home, food, and children. I promise that I shall discharge all my share of the responsibilities for the welfare of the family and the children.*

They continued around the fire seven times in like manner

to complete their vows:

> *Rose, My beloved, now you have walked with me the second step. May the Creator bless you! I will love you and you alone as my wife; I will fill your heart with strength and courage: this is my commitment and my pledge to you. May God protect the lodge and children!*

> *Bob, My husband, at all times I shall fill your heart with courage and strength. In your happiness I shall rejoice. May God bless you and our honorable lodge!*

> *Rose My beloved, now since you have walked three steps with me, our wealth and prosperity will grow. May God bless us! May we educate our children and may they live long.*

> *My husband, I love you with single-minded devotion as my husband. I will treat all other men as my brothers. My devotion to you is pure and you are my joy. This is my commitment and pledge to you.*

> *O' my beloved, it is a great blessing that you have now walked four steps with me. May the Creator bless you! You have brought favor and sacredness in my life.*

O' my husband, in all acts of righteousness, in material prosperity, in every form of enjoyment, and in those divine acts such as fire sacrifice, worship and charity, I promise you that I shall participate and I will always be with you.

O' my beloved, now you have walked five steps with me. May the Creator make us prosperous! May the Creator bless u!.

O' my husband, I will share both in your joys and sorrows. Your love will make me very happy.

O' my beloved, by walking six steps with me, you have filled my heart with happiness. May I fill your heart with great joy and peace, time and time again. May the Creator bless you.

My husband, may the Creator bless you. May I fill your heart with great joy and peace. I promise that 1 will always be with you.

Rose my beloved, as you have walked the seven steps with me, our love and friendship has become inseparable and firm. We have experienced spiritual union in God. Now you have become completely mine. I offer my total self to you. May our marriage last forever.

My husband, by the law of the Creator, and the spirits of our honorable ancestors, I have become your wife. Whatever promises I gave you I have spoken them with a pure heart. All the spirits are witnesses to this fact. I shall never deceive you, nor will I let you down. I shall love you forever.

After the final steps were taken and the last vows were spoken, Bob and Rose shed the blue blankets and were enveloped by relatives in a single white blanket representing their new ways of happiness, fulfillment and peace. Stomp dancers performed for the couple and a prayer of continuance was given by the holy man to end the ceremony.

"God in heaven above please protect the ones we love. We honor all you created as we pledge our hearts and lives together.

We honor mother-earth and ask for this marriage to be abundant and grow stronger through the seasons; we honor fire and ask that their union be warm and glowing with love in our hearts;

We honor wind and ask they sail though life safe and warm as in our father's arms.

We honor water to clean and soothe their relationship; that it may never thirst for love;

With all the forces of the universe
you created, we pray for harmony and
true happiness, as they forever grow
young together.
  Amen."

Bob and Rose drank from a Cherokee Wedding Vase to end the ceremony. The vessel held one drink, but had two openings for the couple to drink at the same time. A great feast followed the ceremony provided by the clans of both families. The dancing and celebrating continued long into the night. After the feast Bob and Rose walked silently and alone to their cabin he had built for her among the clan of the bride's mother as was the custom of their tribe.

John Ross, the friend he called 'Chief' did not attend their wedding, because that same year he was elected chief of the Cherokee nation. The boy that Bob called 'Chief' for the past fifteen years was now really his chief.

As Bob and Rose started their life together, the weeks and months passed quickly, Bob worked his crops and hunted to provide for his new bride. Rose did her part to care for her husband in every way. They both shared a joy that most only dream of, but they both longed for a child. When an Indian couple has a child, the traditional question is, "Is it a bow, or a sifter?" Even at birth, the male is associated with hunting and providing, the female with nourishing and giving life. Their desire for a child was fulfilled in 1829. A violent storm filled the mountains of their community on the eve of the child's birth. The midwives were summoned to for the delivery. Despite their help, Rose had difficulty delivering the child. Although Bob wanted to comfort Rose, he tried not to get in the way and left everything to the women. Things were not going well and he became very concerned. Then a tremendous bolt of lighting and deafening clap of thunder startled Rose and shortly, the child was born. Their child was a 'bow', they named Benjamin. His Indian name was *Unalasgi* or Thunder. His name would be a reminder of this stormy night and would be remembered throughout their life with great joy.

Living in the world of the European settlers made it difficult for Bob and his family to hold onto Cherokee traditions, yet Ben's proud parents tried as best they could to hold on to the ways of their people. Every chance Bob had, he told his children the Cherokee stories and legends that he had heard from his father just as he had heard from his father.

As Bob's farm grew, the work increased and quickly became too much for him to do by himself. Bob sought help with the work only to be reminded of the ways of the settlers. Slavery was widely used and no workers could be found to assist help him on the farm. The only thing Bob could do was to purchase a slave for himself. This was completely against what he believed, but he proceeded with plans to purchase a slave anyway.

Against his better judgment, Bob went to the slave auction to make his purchase. Bob spotted a young man and made arrangement for his purchase. After the purchase was concluded, his new slave Michael, asked, "Would it be alright for me to go and say goodbye to my family?"

Bob was shocked that Michael had a family and expected to be separated from them. How could he separate a man from his family? That would break his heart to cause such a thing?

Bob was a very compassionate man and he replied, "No!

--- That won't be necessary. I'll arrange to purchase them as well. There is nothing more valuable than a man's family. Your family must stay together!"

Michael had a wife and two sons that would became excellent workers. Michael and his family were the only slaves purchased by Bob. Michael cost Bob one of his best horses. Michael's family cost Bob another of his workhorses and one of his riding horses. The transaction was far more costly than Bob had anticipated, but he knew he had done the right thing keeping Michael's family together. As the wagons were loaded for the trip home, Bob still didn't feel right about owning a man and his family.

So from the beginning Bob told Michael, "You are a free man and not a slave, consider yourself a sharecropper. If you ever feel mistreated, I will grant your freedom. And you and your family will be free to go."

"Yes sir, Mr. Mace. I be a free man!" For his freedom, Michael remained loyal to Bob. Michael's family grew as they worked along side Bob and his family. Michael and his family worked hard for Bob. They were well provided for and always treated with dignity.

Bob's son, Ben, grew into manhood in his father's footsteps. That was literally true in one case. When Ben was about seven years old he and his father were in the woods hunting. It was early spring and a recent rain left the ground soggy and muddy. As Bob walked along he left footprints in the mud, Ben followed close behind trying to make big steps and walk in his father's tracks. Bob noticed what was happening and without Ben's knowledge he began to take smaller steps making it easier for Ben to follow. Ben would have kept-up no matter how difficult it might have been. Ben thought his dad was the greatest man to ever live. As they sat down to have a cool drink from the creek, Ben asked his papa to tell him a story. This is something that Bob did often in hopes of keeping the Cherokee traditions alive for his family.

"Papa, tell me a story that you have never told me!"

Bob thought for a moment and started his story. "There is a battle of two wolves in every person. One is evil and is always anger, envious and jealous. He brings sorrow, regret, greed, arrogance, self-pity, lies, false pride, superiority, and ego. The other is good and he is joyful and peaceful. He is always about love, hope, serenity, humility, kindness, generosity, truth, compassion and faith."

"Which wolf wins"? The son asks.

The dad responds, "That is a very good question … my answer is, the one that you feed….." If Ben asked for a story, Bob was always ready to tell one with life principals.

With the discovery of gold on Cherokee land, the doom of the Cherokee was sealed. The political folks in Washington had decreed that the Indians must be moved west and their lands given to the whites. In a few short years their lives were to change forever. As those years progressed, the Cherokee's plight was not improving and Chief John Ross asked Bob to remain in Tennessee and help for a while. In March of 1837, Bob summoned Michael and his family to his home.

"Mr. Mace, why have you asked us to your home?"

"Michael, I have a great favor to ask of you. I told you many years ago, that you were a free man. Things are not going well for my people here and I want to take my family to Arkansas.

However, I have committed to John Ross to remain here 'til our tribes future is determined and I need you to take them, you and your family are welcome to stay here if you desire, but I trust you to safely deliver my family to Arkansas. Remember our neighbor, John Lane moved there some time back and sent me this map. He says there is good farmland there."

"Mr. Mace, I will do as you ask and I will take my family there also. You gave me my freedom, but my place is in your service, now and always."

"Thanks, you'll never know what this means to me."

In the days ahead, Bob and Michael made plans for the move. Bob's property was sold for far less than it was worth, but more than necessary to purchase property in Arkansas. Additional wagons were purchased as well for the journey. The day for trip to begin was a very sad day. Bob and Rose had been constant companions since their marriage. The most they had ever been apart was a few days when he would attend tribal council meetings. Facing uncertain times he didn't know when they might be reunited. Rose was expecting their fourth child as they set out for Arkansas. Ben was eight, Drew seven, and six-year-old Frances joined the others for the trip west. They had ten wagons loaded with all their possessions. March 15, 1837 Michael departed North Carolina bound for Arkansas with Bob's family and his as well. Bob's decision to send his family ahead proved to be a good one based on the events and hardships that were to come in 1838.

April 10, 1837

To My Friend, Chief John Ross,

I want you to know that I, as well as our people appreciate all the work you have done in order to save our homes and the lands of our fathers. Even though your father is Scottish and your mother is Cherokee, the Cherokee traditions run deep in your soul. Your work has always been in the best interest of the Cherokee people. As the first elected chief of our people, your work has been first and foremost for the Cherokee Nation and their interests. It is with great pride that I count you as my friend. It gives me great honor to serve a Chief such as you. It appears that your work has not turned out as we had hoped. If we do not relocate our people, I fear that we will be forced to leave this place we have called home for many years. I will continue to work with you in hopes that a settlement can be reached with the government. You will always have my support and the support of my family. Life has been wonderful for both of our families here in the Smoky Mountains. We have thrived in business and obtained great wealth, both in money and in friendships. My prayer is for a continued life here, but I have planned for the worst. I have sent my trusted friend, Michael, to Arkansas to purchase land for me there. I am sending Rose and my family with him. I will join you in Tennessee and will remain there until our fate is resolved. No matter what happens our friendship will never change .I will see you soon.

Your Friend,
Bob Mace

TRAIL OF TEARS

Nunna daul Isunyi "the Trail Where They Cried".

Relocation of the tribe

A small group of Cherokee Chiefs signed the Treaty of New Echota. They claimed to represent the council and have its approval to make the treaty, but that was not true. The council had explicitly voted against this group having any authority.

In May the first of seven groups was taken to Oklahoma before the forced removal began. The last of these groups left in October. These seven groups included many of the wealthy mixed-blood Cherokee and many of the signers of the Treaty of New Echota. The signers of this treaty gladly left fearing for their lives and rightly so. In June of 1839 Major Ridge, his son John Ridge and Elias Boudinot, three signers of that treaty, were assassinated. Several others were also killed later starting a wave of violence across the Cherokee nation. Tribal divisions were exacerbated by the outbreak of the Civil War.

John Ross met with General Winfield Scott in Washington in mid-May about the removal. Later, Ross was able to get Scott to agree to several requests for the Cherokees.

However, before Ross returned home on May 25, 1838, Scott's soldiers rounded up all the Cherokees from their homes and imprisoned them in three stockades. These in Tennessee were at Cleveland, Calhoun and Ross' Landing. The agreements Ross and Scott had made were not honored by the general. When Ross returned home, his people were already imprisoned in the three stockades.

November 1838

My Dear Rose,

It has been over a year since I sent you to Arkansas with Michael. A year's absence from you is almost more than I can bear. And yet I am glad you are not here, but safe in a new place. I don't know if word has reached you about our condition here. In May soldiers began a round up of our people. We have been placed in a stockade at Ross' Landing and I fear that I might not see you again at least for a time. Soldiers under the command of General Winfield Scott marched into our town gathering our people and placing us in pens. This will surely be remembered as one of the darkest days of the Cherokee people. We, including John Ross and his family, were rounded-up like cattle and placed in camps or stockades until our relocation could be finalized. As the soldiers entered our homes, they began knocking over pots and looking for anything of value to steal. Anger and frustration filled my heart, but I was powerless to resist the force of the soldiers. We were forced to leave everything behind. All we had was what we were wearing on that day.

As each day passes, more and more people are herded into the stockades. The numbers in the camps grow larger with each day. As new groups arrive, news of what is happening on the outside is exchanged with us. The elders of the tribe are anxious and the mothers fearful, however the children still attempted to play.

As the days grow into weeks and weeks to months, whites have moved into our homes and began farming our lands. Conditions are terrible for us, yet no one wants to leave the mountains that have been home for so many years. As fall approaches, the stockade is nothing more than mud and we can't remember when we were last clean. With winter here, it has become very cold and it is difficult for us stay warm. There are a few blankets but many more people to warm than a few blankets can provide. Mothers clutched their young in their arms in a futile attempt to keep them warm. They were driven from their homes barefooted with poor clothing and no blankets to help keep warm.

There is a young soldier here that has offered his help in getting word to you. I would like to tell you his name, but he told me that he is one-quarter Cherokee and is fearful that he will be found out. I disparately pray for an escape from this place, for our people and me. However, we wait to learn of our fate and it looks as if we are going to have to suffer the cold winter here. We have little to warm ourselves. Blankets are few and we have little to eat. I miss you and the family at this time of thanksgiving. With all that is going on here it is difficult to be thankful. However, I am thankful that you and the children are safe and not enduring the hardships of our people here. John is not hopeful that the situation is going to improve and he is very discouraged. He feels he has let our people down and I can offer no help or encouragement. I was planning to leave here in the spring, but the soldiers put a stop to that.

I hope my young friend is able to get this letter to you. Give my love to the children and a kind word to Michael and his family. I am sure that you rely on him greatly in my absence. Should I not be able to return to you, know that only death shall prevent it. God willing, I will see you again.

  Your loving husband,

  Bob

Just as sudden as the horror of the captivity had begun, an even greater horror was to follow. The forced removal began on the first day of the tenth month of 1838 as the guards came to the stockade and the Cherokees were led out of their prison. The Indians were divided into three groups. Each of the three groups was taken in smaller groups of about a thousand each to the west. In the middle of winter the task of relocation of the Cherokee people had begun. Why was it decided to make the move now? Already the chill of winter was beginning to fill the air. Why not wait until spring? October 1, 1838, John Benge took the first of the Cherokee controlled parties from Tennessee through Missouri, Arkansas, and to Oklahoma. General Winfield Scott rode to Nashville with this group. When they arrived in Oklahoma, they had only twenty-seven casualties. Seven other groups left in early October. The number in these groups totaled 6,583 and 331 were added along the way. Their losses were heavy, 894, and only 6,020 Cherokees arrived in Oklahoma. November 4, 1838, Peter Hildebrand led a group along a northern watercourse with 1,776 Cherokee, by the time they arrived in Oklahoma 464 Cherokees had perished and buried along the trail. As the Cherokee walked across the frozen ground, the bitter cold filled their bodies. The provisions had not been improved and the Indians still had few blankets to warm their bodies. The soldiers had their heavy coats and blankets to keep themselves warm at night. Only a very few of the soldiers had sympathy for the Indians, but they were not allowed to help. Disease and sickness over took many of the tribe. As their condition grew worse many died. This scene was repeated until all of the people were removed and relocated in Oklahoma. What was the crime of these proud Cherokee? What evil had they done to be placed in these camps? The Cherokee had lived on these lands for hundreds of years. When the Europeans came, the Cherokee welcomed them to their land with open arms and shared their land with the settlers. What evil possessed these settlers to turn on their gracious neighbors? Had the lure of gold discovered on Cherokee land caused such greed to possess the settlers? In less than half a century the settlers had turn on the owners of this land. Had the friendship of the Indians brought this treatment on the proud Cherokee people? This forced removal was to become known as 'The Trail of Tears'

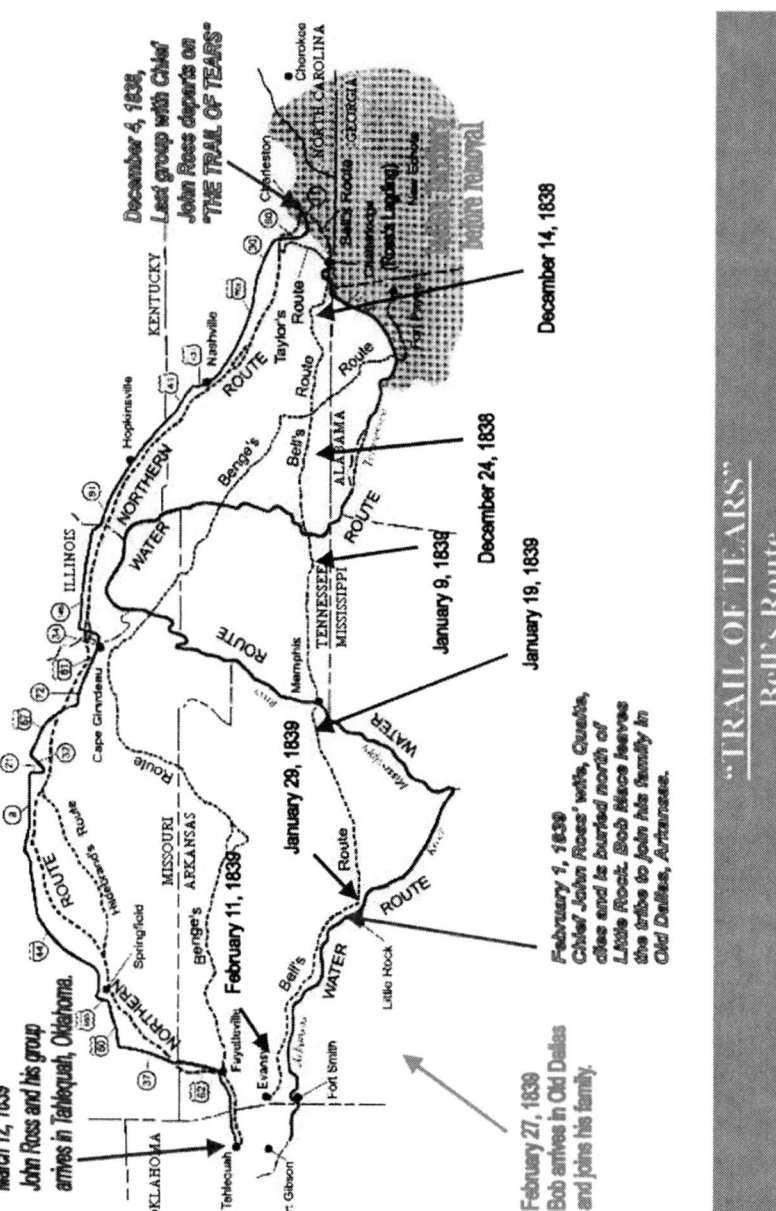

"TRAIL OF TEARS"
Bell's Route

The Trail of Tears begins

John Ross had hoped to spend Christmas at home before leaving on the long journey to the Indian Territory in Oklahoma, However that was not to be. As the soldiers gathered this last group, John Ross led his people in prayer with Bob Mace at his side, when the bugle sounded the wagons started rolling. Children rose to their feet and waved good-by to their mountain homes, not knowing they were leaving them forever. Mothers wept at the sight of their disappearing homeland in the distance. Men were angered by the injustice done to their families. John Ross left the Cherokee homeland carrying the records and laws of the Cherokee nation and little else.

The last party left on December 4, 1838. This third detachment, conducted by John Bell and administered by U.S. Army Lt. Edward Deas made its way through southern Tennessee, Arkansas, and on to Oklahoma. Bob Mace was included in Bell's group as was the chief and his wife, Elizabeth 'Quatie' Brown Henley. This group was the last to leave the mountains the Cherokee had called home for hundreds of years and the only group to follow this southern route. The Bell route started near Ross Landing, a community established by John Ross and traveled due west, crossing the Mississippi River and up the north bank of the Arkansas River to Ft. Gibson, Indian Territory. The first group started the journey months earlier and by November 1838, twelve groups of 1,000 were trudging 800 miles overland to the west. Hundreds of heavily loaded Conestoga covered wagons on the muddy trails caused by heavy autumn rains made them impassable.

The first week of travel for Bell's group was harsh and they covered less than a hundred miles. Lt. Deas ordered them to push harder and march longer each day. John Ross had requested permission from General Scott for his people to be allowed to search the woods along the way for food. Because the group was small, General Scott granted his permission. However, with the harshness of the winter, little was found to help feed John Ross' people.

Week two was no different from the first. Travel was slow and provisions low. However, things were getting worse. The Indian's physical condition was weak and their resistance to disease was low. At the beginning of the third week, they suffered their first loss. An elderly couple failed to answer the morning wake-up call. Weakened by sickness and age they were not able to withstand the harsh winter night. They were found clutching each other in an attempt to keep warm. However, their survival was not to be and they journeyed to meet their Maker arm in arm. The couple was buried along the trail by the tribe.

Chief John Ross spoke a word to his people at the service. "Today we lost two of our elders. All of us will miss them. The chill of the night took them from us and they now enjoy the warmth of the Creator's arms. May the Creator keep them warm and protect us this day. Amen."

By Christmas day Bell's group was approaching the Tennessee River. Bob wanted to forget it all, but the picture of their wagons lumbering over the frozen ground with their cargo of suffering people lingered in his mind. The journey ahead for his people held much more suffering and hardships. Many were sick from their confinement that started many months before their departure. During confinement they had little food, no medical care and their dwellings were shabby at best and very cold. What little they had been able to bring with them, was often stolen and sold by the soldiers. This last group was the smallest and had some of the very old and the very young. It was difficult for these to withstand the conditions that faced them. Not only were they sick and weak they still had only a few blankets for warmth and provisions were scarce.

As their wagons approached a community, the town's people came out to witness the caravan of Cherokees. Bob felt like his people were a sideshow in a circus, like animals on display. Many of the town's people had sympathy for the Indians and others were glad to see them being relocated. A few of these settlers had problems with the Indians in the past and for that reason feared them. They felt safer with the Indians no longer as neighbors, even though the Cherokees had been good neighbors for many years. Some of the town's people shed tears and others offered jeers.

During January two-thirds of the Cherokees were trapped between the ice-bound Ohio and Mississippi Rivers. With provisions low more people became sick and died. During the latter part of January, Bob encountered a young boy about ten or eleven years old. Bob's thoughts returned to the memory of his son and the rest of his family. The boy was alone and frightened.

Bob had compassion for this boy and asked, "What is your name?"

The lad responded, "My name is Samuel but, I call myself *Sadness*. I have lost my family. --- My father was the first to die. Soon after my mother became sick and she died too. I had three brothers and two sisters and they all died. I am the only one of my family to survive. *"*

Fighting back tears, Bob replied, "I am so sorry to hear that. I have a son about your age. He is not with me. ---- He is safe in Arkansas with the rest of my family. If you would like to stay with me while we journey on, it would please me very much." Bob's plan or his dream, if they survived this ordeal and he was reunited with his family, was to take this boy into his family. This was the ancient tradition of the Cherokee people. When a child was orphaned, they would be taken in another in the clan. Many clans we in the group and the boy's clan was not known.

Samuel agreed and the two traveled together for a several days. Despite the hardships of their journey, the children remained playful. About a week later *Sadness* was playing with another young boy and *Sadness* told him about the ordeal of losing his family. The family of the other boy was moved by his story and asked *Sadness* to join them. It was good for the boy to be back in family environment and it made *Sadness* feel a little better and at least he was not so alone any longer. After that *Sadness* again used his given name, Samuel. Bob was happy that Samuel had found a new friend and good family.

As February approached, the Chief's wife became ill. Although suffering from a cold, Quatie Ross gave her blanket to a child freezing from the cold. Bob found another old blanket and gave it to Quatie. Without ever warming herself, she passed the blanket on to another cold child. John and Bob pleaded with her to keep a blanket, but she replied, "As long as one child suffers, I can not warm myself." As a result Quatie's condition worsened and she died of pneumonia on the first day of February 1839 near Monnie Springs in Arkansas.

After Quatie's funeral John Ross pleaded with Bob to escape from the tribe and make his way to his family in Arkansas. Bob agreed and managed to slip away from the tribe undetected. No one knows how many of the reported four thousand casualties suffered by the Cherokee actually managed to slip from away the tribe as Bob had done.

Bob left with little more than the clothes on his back. Chief John Ross provided him with all that he could, a little beef jerky and some water. Bob was headed home, a place he had never seen before. He was following the hand drawn map his neighbor, John Lane, had sent him before the round up of the Cherokees. From Monnie Springs, Bob traveled west to the Fourche LaFave River and then along the river. By the end of the third day, the jerky was almost gone. Being next to the river, he always had plenty of water. Bob lost his map in the river about a week later and had to rely on his memory of the map and was unsure how to proceed. As so many others of the tribe, the ordeal of his confinement in the stockades and trip during the harsh winter left Bob in poor health. He became very weak, he was sure he was about to die and he prepared to meet his Maker.

O' my Creator you are so gracious to me. You have delivered my family safely to Arkansas and brought safe me this far; I have lost my map and don't have the strength to continue. The bitter cold fills my bones and I feel my end is near. Continue to bless my family and provide them comfort with my loss. Amen.

With the conclusion of his prayer everything went white and he slipped into a deep sleep. He was sure that he had died, but when he woke up, the first thing he saw was a dead rabbit about a foot in front of his face. Just on the other side of the rabbit was a hawk perched on a rock near by. The hawk looked into Bob's eyes as if to say *this is for you.* Bob started a fire, cooked the rabbit and regained some strength. Bob set up a camp for a few days to rest and trap some game for food. Bob noticed that the hawk did not leave and was always nearby. Bob made a bow and some arrows from the limited items at his disposal. He trapped a few rabbits and after skinning and drying them he continued on his way. The Chief had a knife that his father brought from Scotland and the Chief gave it to Bob when he left the tribe. With the bow made from an oak limb and a strip of leather cut from his buckskin coat, some simple but effective arrows, and the knife of the Chief, Bob was able to keep a supply of food and always had plenty of water. His biggest problem was keeping warm and which direction to travel. As he broke camp to continue his journey, he hesitated as he considered which trail to take. He started off in one direction and the hawk came back and landed in his path. Bob tried to go around the hawk and the hawk flapped his wings and would not let Bob pass. The hawk flew a few feet to another trail and Bob followed until nightfall. Each morning when Bob woke-up, the hawk was there, sometimes with food and other times only to say good morning. Bob followed the hawk as it chose the direction of travel each day. Bob took this hawk to be a messenger from God. He and the hawk continued to follow the river for about two weeks, stopping only to rest and replenish his food supply. Bob continued to followed the hawk and during the third week they left the riverbanks and started southwest through the Ouachita Mountains. March was approaching and the weather was becoming more bearable. Each day he followed the hawk and was covering much more distance now away from the tribe.

By March 12, 1839, Chief John Ross and all Cherokee survivors had arrived in their destination in what is now eastern Oklahoma. No one knows how many died throughout the ordeal, but the trip was especially hard on infants, children, and the elderly. A missionary doctor by the name of Elizur Butler accompanied the Cherokees on 'The Trail of Tears'. He estimated that over four thousand died, or nearly a fifth of the Cherokee population. Four thousand silent graves reaching from the foothills of the Smoky Mountains to what is known as Indian Territory in the west were left along 'The Trail of Tears' and covetousness on the part of the white settlers was the cause of all that the Cherokees had suffered.

August 1839, John Ross was elected Principal Chief of the reconstituted Cherokee Nation. Tahlequah, Oklahoma was named its capital. John Ross remained their chief until his death August 1, 1866.

LIFE GOES ON
Mena, Arkansas

John F. Lane and his wife, Catherine 'Kitty' Ballinger, were part of a Quaker family that came to America from England before the Revolutionary War. The Lane family settled in Guilford County, North Carolina, near Bob and his family. Later the Lane family migrated west to Arkansas. John's family first settled near the Old Potter community farming 500 acres of land on Old Line Road, about five miles southwest of Mena, Arkansas. After their housed burned, they moved to Old Dallas, the county seat of Polk County. John later served in the Arkansas House of Representatives in 1871 as a representative from the thirteenth district.

Michael had arrived in Arkansas June 8, 1837 with the two families. He acquired 240 acres adjacent to the Lane's property for Bob. As soon as they arrived, work on a new farm started. Starting a new farm was difficult work. Michael, his family, about twenty others, and Bob's family had been in Arkansas working for over a year and waiting for Bob to arrive. Their last news from Bob was Thanksgiving of 1838. Although they had no word from Bob for many months, they continued clearing the fields of timber, building new houses and planting crops in anticipation of his arrival. The work took time and lots of hard work, but their lives were much better than the life faced by those on the reservation. They worked long hours every day except, Sunday. Even though Bob's family held on to Cherokee traditions, they had become Christians and adopted the faith of their European neighbors back in North Carolina. They always had a time of Thanksgiving and worship each week.

Early in the afternoon of March 4, 1839 the hawk Bob was following landed on the roof of a farmhouse off in the distance. This beautiful spring day warmed Bob's tired aching body and he knew he was home at last. The sight of the house with smoke rising from the chimney made the day even more gorgeous. As he approached the house, he saw all the men in the fields working. A woman was alone in the house preparing food for the evening meal when she spotted a man approaching house. Not knowing the man was her husband she picked up the shotgun and stood behind the closed door. Bob knocked weakly on the door, She threw open the door and before Bob could speak, he collapsed into the room. Rose took her husband, exhausted from his many months of traveling and enduring the rough winter and placed him in a warm bed where he remained for several days. When he got out of bed, he learned that his son, Drew, had been killed in an accident during the family's trip to Arkansas. Even though weary and saddened from the news of son's death, he was glad to be inside a warm cabin and with his family. He went outside the house for the first time since his arrival for some fresh and air. He took a hot cup of coffee, his first in over two years and he was enjoying every drop. He was sitting in his favorite rocker and shortly heard the sound of rustling wings as the hawk flew from over the house and landed on the rail in front of him. The hawk peered into Bob's eyes and he could sense the hawk was leaving. Bob responded verbally, *"Thanks old friend, I know the Creator sent you to lead me home and your work is done. Thanks to Him and you for my deliverance."* With his words spoken, the hawk flapped his wings and took off. He circled the yard in front of Bob several times and started a spiral upward, climbing higher and higher and vanished into the distant clouds.

The following Sunday there was a great celebration by his family and the others that came from North Carolina. Bob was asked to speak to the members of their small country church about his ordeal. Most of the members were white, but a few were Cherokee. Bob choose his words carefully so that he would not show hard feelings for the whites that caused the suffering of his people, but his words did conveyed the horror and hardships they encountered. Bob could have become a bitter person because of 'The Trail of Tears', but he didn't. He felt the experience left him wiser and stronger.

Bob told the congregation, "Adversity builds character and this experience made me a better man. It didn't kill me. It may have weakened my body, but it did not weaken my spirit. The Creator provided for me then and He will now as well. Thank you for letting me speak to you today."

The Cherokee were moved by his experience and the whites felt shame for what the soldiers and whites had done to Bob's people. After church they all, Cherokee and whites alike, gathered for an old fashion church picnic. Every one of the white members approached Bob and one by one apologized to him for the actions of the whites. Bob told them that no apology was necessary because they themselves had done nothing wrong. He said they should not be ashamed for others wrongdoings.

As Ben grew older, he became more and more like his father. His features matched his father almost exactly. Strangers often confused them for brothers. Bob seemed ageless despite the damage the journey had done to his body. He taught Ben the same skills his father had taught him, hunting, fishing, and farming. But, more important than these skills, he taught his son the values of being a good and honest man. With love and nurturing from his father Ben gained his father's gentle nature and wisdom.

The neighbors of Bob and Rose had a daughter a year younger than Ben. Susannah Stanton was not the typical young lady. Ben first saw her as he was hunting for deer. Ben thought she was a boy at first. She was dressed in jeans and a buckskin coat. Her hair was concealed under her hat and she was in the woods alone practicing shooting or hunting as Ben first thought. As Ben approached her, she turned her rifle toward him. He noticed that this boy had very delicate features and he quickly stated that he meant no harm. When this lad removed his hat, he could tell why the features were so delicate; this boy was a very fine looking girl. However, she was small and frail looking even for girl. The Stanton's were not Indian and Susannah was very different from the other girls Ben knew. Her skin was fair and had hair the color of wheat ready for harvest. Her eyes were green that would change to a shade of blue with the reflection of the blue sky. Her eyes reminded him of the clear water of a mountain pond. It was love at first sight for Ben. Susannah however had to be convinced over the next several years that Ben was indeed her soul mate.

Susannah paid no mind to Ben over the years until she was kidnapped at the age of fifteen and held for ransom. Susannah's father was a very wealthy man and somewhat ruthless and not particularly liked by some in the community. He had a few enemies in the area and a couple of the town's undesirable sought to make a profit from the capture of his daughter. Before a ransom demand could be made, Ben tracked her captors to their hiding place, an abandoned farm house about five miles from the Stanton farm. Ben returned home and told his dad where Susannah was being held. Susannah's father, Ben and his father along with several neighbors went to rescue Susannah. The two men were surprised and captured before they harmed Susannah. Justice was swift in those days and the two were hanged on the spot. Susannah was removed from the scene and taken home before the hanging, but Ben remained and witnessed the swift justice or more likely injustice. Ben was a gentle young man as was his father and the sight of this event lingered with him for the rest of his life. Ben's father had pleaded with the others not to hang the men, but to give them a trial. Ben admired his father for trying to do the right thing. That event and a desire for fair judgment led Ben into law enforcement later in life. As his father had, he believed the two should have had a trial before they were executed. Susannah realized that Ben may have very well have saved her life that day.

From that day on Ben was committed to protecting Susannah. And she was not opposed to his protection. When you saw one the other was certain to be close by. Their bond had been formed and their relationship was something everyone in town knew was going to happen for a long time. Ben and Susannah's parents saw how perfect they were suited for each other and were very happy for the youngsters. Even though she was not Cherokee, Ben followed their customs for marriage. He asked for her hand, built a house for her and their future family. After a year's courtship Ben married Susannah in 1850. Ben was the first in his family to marry outside the tribe. Even though Susannah wasn't Indian, she and Ben continued to follow the Indian traditions, but broke from the custom of the husband becoming part of the wife's clan. Instead Ben built a house on his dad's property about a mile from his parent's house.

During the early days of their marriage, Ben settled into his new life with his bride in the foothills of the Ouachita Mountains. The newly weds began to explore the wilderness of their surroundings and often shared the seclusion together. Other times Ben went alone, except for his dog. It was during these times of seclusion that his soul was rekindled with the wonder of God's creation and oneness with the Creator. He found that his questions were answered here. These questions and answers seemed to be unimportant with a terrible discovery he made during one of his solo explorations. He came upon a campsite and found the bodies of two men. Ben was glad the Susannah wasn't with him. The bodies had begun to decompose and animals had torn into their flesh feeding on the bodies. It was not a pleasant scene. Ben figured they had been dead less than a month. The two men had been shot in the head and appeared there had been no struggle with the shooter or shooters. Any supplies or animals they may have had were missing and only the partial bodies remained. They were not deep into the wilderness and not to far from Ben's house. He returned home and reported his finding to one of their neighbor, John Lane. The community had no sheriff and John told him to forget about it. John's advice didn't set well with Ben. Even though there was no sheriff, two men had died and someone should find out who killed them. Ben couldn't let go of the image of the two men and felt compelled to find the motive and the identity of the killer or killers, even if no one else cared. Ben took it upon himself and his career as a law officer had just begun. Ben began to ask question of the people in the area and they were hesitant to help at first. However, he was persistent and they began to open up to him. They were actually glad that someone cared enough to investigate this murder. He learned that two men came through the area sometime earlier and spent an evening at *The Peach Tree*. Jacob Schwarzkopf ran this small tavern at the edge of town and some of the local men went there to drink, gamble, and involve themselves with other illicit activities. Jacob or Jake as everyone called him was the law at *The Peach Tree* and under Jake's law everything was legal. *The Peach Tree* was well known in the area for the activities there. Ben didn't like the idea of going there, but to continue his investigation he had no choice. Jake was a big burley man of German descent and made his own brew from an old family recipe. Jake stood six feet-four inches and weight almost three hundred pounds. His face was weathered and red from years of drinking his homemade brew. Jake didn't like Ben coming around asking question any more than Ben liked being there. Ben had not been at *The Peach Tree* long before Jake noticed him asking questions.

"Hey you, get out of here and stop botherin' my customer." Jake shouted from behind the bar. Jake's demand went unheeded. Jake, being of superior size, approached Ben and was going to force Ben to leave. That was Jake's first mistake.

"Mr. Schwarzkopf, I'm only trying to investigate a murder and I don't mean to bother you or your customers. As soon as I get answers to my questions, I will gladly leave." Ben responded.

"Boy, I told you to leave and I mean now!" as Jake grabbed Ben's arm and started pulling him toward the door. Ben took hold of Jake's hand and pushed him. Ben was very strong his shove slammed Jake hard against the wall. The jolt knocked the wind out of Jake for a moment. When he regained his wind Jake made his second mistake and pulled his knife. Ben never carried a pistol, only a rifle and his trusty knife. Ben's rifle was outside on his saddle because he had not expected trouble that night. Before Jake could make a move, Ben drew his knife with lightning speed and without hesitation sent his knife in Jake's direction. Ben's knife buried deep into the wall behind Jake. The knife was under Jake's right arm, pinning him to wall by his shirt.

Jake was stunned to be pinned to the wall and stood there looking at the knife under his arm and said, "What are you doing? You could have killed me!"

Ben responded, "My knife found its mark, if I had wanted to kill you, you would be dead now. All I want is your cooperation." Ben's dog was showing his teeth to any other would be attacker. Blue was a mixed breed dog, part English Shepard and many believed part wolf. He was a very large dog, gentle for the most part but, very protective of his master. Blue was a gift from Chief John Ross and was Ben's constant companion. Now that Ben had the undivided attention of Jake, maybe he could get some answers.

Jake was a bit more cooperative now as he spoke, "Okay, two strangers were here about two months ago. They drank a lot and began bragging about gold they found in Georgia. I don't think they found it on their claim, but someone else's claim. I say that because the men said they left with their gold before the law could catch them. So it must not have been theirs"

Ben thought to himself, the gold was probably Cherokee gold that his people were not allowed to mine. But that was a different story.

"The men spent the evening here drinking and gambling." Jake continued.

Ben asked, "Did the two men lose or win that night?"

"I don't keep-up with that; things are pretty lose around here. I just serve drinks and let everybody have a good time. But, I do think they won some money that night."

"Do you know who lost money that night?" Ben responded.

"I don't keep-up with names. Everybody lost some, some more than others." Jake then lowered his voice to a whisper, "These locals thought the two strangers were cheating and they probably were, but I allowed them to continuing playing. It's not difficult to cheat these men; they're simple farmers out for a night of fun and not good card players. The two men left and I haven't seen them since."

"Mr. Schwarzkopf thanks for you help --- and I'm sorry about the knife incident."

"Well, I'm not used to anyone standing up to me, besides I could see I was no match for you and that dog. I could use a dog like that here. I have to respect you for standing your ground."

"Thanks and again I am sorry for the knife thing!"

The next day Ben went to Tweeter's General Store to continue his investigation. Bevis McCahill, the owner of the store, was a tiny man of Scottish descent. He still spoke with an accent in a very high-pitched voice. Everyone thought he sounded like a bird, so he had been called Tweeter all of his life. News of Ben's night at *The Peach Tree* traveled fast in the small community and Tweeter was eager to help with Ben's investigation. The entire town was glad to hear that he had stood up to Jake and thankful someone was interested in bringing some law to the area. Jake was the town's tough guy and no one had ever stood their ground with him. Ben's action brought him instant respect in the community and near hero status.

Tweeter spoke to Ben as he entered the store, "Good morning Ben. I heard 'bout what happened at *The Peach Tree* last night. The whole town is abuzz this mornin' 'bout it."

"News travels fast in these parts, doesn't it?" Ben replied.

"Good news does for sure. What can I do for you this morning?" Tweeter asked.

"Jake told me that two men had been in his place bragging about some gold they had. Have you heard any stories of gold lately?" Ben asked.

"Well, I haven't heard any stories about gold, but one of my customers came in a few weeks ago and paid his long overdue bill with gold. His name is Sam Jenkins. Everybody knows Sam was no good as a farmer and his wife left him years ago, she and their kids went back east. Sam had a new team of horses hitched to a wagon. I asked him where he got the gold and wagon. He said he won them gambling at *The Peach Tree*. Sam couldn't win a spittin' contest, let alone a game of cards. He was on edge and appeared to be scared. The wagon was full with everything he owned. After paying his bill he headed west out of town."

"Thanks Tweeter, that helps me a lot. --- See ya later."

That night Ben returned to *The Peach Tree* to inquire of Sam's presence there the night the two strangers were there. Jake noticed Ben as he came in.

Jake spoke before Ben closed the door, "Good evening, what brings you back tonight?"

"Mr. Schwarzkopf ---"

Before Ben could say another word, Jake spoke, "Boy, call me Jake, everybody else does. When you say Mr. Schwarzkopf, I look around for my worthless father."

"OK, I'll call you Jake --- and just for the record, Ben is my name, not *Boy*"

"Yes, OK now that we have been properly introduced, what I can I do for you tonight?"

Ben asked, "Do you remember if Sam Jenkins was here the night the strangers were?"

Jake thought for a moment before replying, "Can't say for sure, but I think he was. Yes, I do remember, he was here that night. Yes, I remember he was playing cards with the men."

"Did he lose much money that night?" Ben asked.

"Sam didn't have much to lose and like I told you before, these farmers ain't good card players. Sam didn't win anything."

"Can you tell me anything else?"

"After the two men won all of Sam's money, they left; Sam had one more drink for the road, on credit. --- I don't normally give these farmers credit, but I guess I was feeling sorry for him, but don't let that get around."

"Your secret is safe with me. Thanks for your help, maybe

our paths will cross again."

Ben presented his finding to the town council at the next meeting.

The spokesman for the council said, "Ben thanks for your work. We are glad that you were led to investigate. Your evidence is convincing and we believe Sam is guilty just as you say."

"I would like to go after Sam and bring him back for trial." Ben said.

"Ben --- we understand your desire to go after him, but we are not able to conduct a legal trial. I for one feel you have done enough. Sam has been gone for several weeks and no one is sure where he was headed. Sam is not around any more, we're glad the murder has been solved and the murderer is out of our area."

Afterward the council met briefly, then the spokesman continued, "Ben, There is just one other thing. The council and I would like you to be our sheriff. We can't pay you just now, but we need someone to provide a little law and order here. We feel you are the man for the job"

Ben looked over at Susannah and she nodded her approval. Ben said, "Yes, I will be glad to serve as sheriff, if that is the desire of everyone."

Almost the entire town was at the meeting. The spokesman called for a show of hands, Ben was elected sheriff without a dissenting vote. The memory of the hanging after Susannah's rescue had given him a great sense for justice and everyone knew his honesty and compassion for the people. Ben had a great sense for the truth and could spot a lie quicker than anyone. One of his favorite expressions was, "I can tell when someone is pissin' on my moccasins and tellin' me it's rainin'."

Ben's new duties as sheriff didn't change his life much. There was little to do since most of the town's people were honest and hard working. Jake even cleaned up *The Peach Tree* to some degree. Life was simple and Ben was able to spend a lot of time with his family.

Ben and his dog had been companions since they both were pups. One night in the fall of 1850, Ben heard a terrible commotion outside the cabin. There was a full moon that night and he could easily see what was going on. He looked out the window and he saw Blue fighting with a fox. The next morning, Ben took Blue into the woods and shot him. Ben knew that a fox would not come close to the cabin, much less fight with a dog four times his size unless something was wrong with him. The fox surely had rabies to do something like that. Blue was sure to catch rabies from his wounds inflected during the fight. The only thing Ben could do was to put him down. Ben buried Blue near by in the woods they both loved. Ben told friends later it was one of the hardest things he ever had to do! That year for Christmas Susannah gave Ben a new puppy. Ben named him Banjo. Banjo was a smaller breed dog of mixed breed, the mother was a beagle and the father was an English Spaniel. Banjo was nothing like Blue and Ben was glad of that. However, he quickly became attached to Banjo. Banjo was his constant companion just as Blue had been. He spent a lot of time with Banjo and during those times taught him many tricks. One of Ben's favorite tricks to amuse his friends was to place a biscuit on Banjo's nose. The dog would sit there with the biscuit on his nose until he got the okay from his master. Then and only then, Banjo flipped the biscuit into the air, catch and eat it before it hit the ground. If Banjo missed the biscuit, he wouldn't eat it off the ground. Banjo never ate a biscuit that had been placed on his nose until Ben gave the okay. One summer afternoon, Ben and his buddies were sharing some old tales and Ben placed a biscuit on Banjo's nose and then got side tracked telling one his famous stories. Banjo sat there for over thirty minutes with that biscuit on his nose. Ben finally noticed Banjo sitting with the biscuit on his nose. Ben and his friends laughed, then Ben gave the nod and Banjo finally got his biscuit.

Susannah was very sick during the winter of 1850 and Ben thought she was going to die. She remained in bed for most of the winter and Ben left her side only when it could not be avoided. His duties as sheriff were not demanding and he spent a lot of time with her. Susannah must have thought she was going to die also. Ben read to her every day from the only book they had. Ben read from Proverbs and Psalms from the Bible.

In early January of 1851, Susannah said, "Ben, we've had a good life together haven't we?"

"Yes, we have and we are goin' to have a lot more of it."

"I pray that is so, but I feel my time is short. I'm sorry that we never had the children that we both wanted so badly. After I die, you will find love again. Marry her and have the family that you always wanted. I'm sorry that I was unable to give you any children."

"Susannah, my precious love, don't talk like that. You're goin' to be fine. You'll be up and around in no time. Just wait and see!"

"Ben, you've made me so happy during the time we've had together. Please just remember what I have told you, marry, be happy, and go on with life."

Susannah did recover that winter, but she had always been frail and in the winter of 1851 she became ill again and past away January 17, 1852. She was only twenty-three years old. Ben became withdrawn and spent a lot of time in the wilderness with Banjo. Before Susannah died, Ben developed a fondness for racing horses and his were the finest and fastest in the area. The town gatherings often centered on horse racing. Ben's horses never lost. But, after Susannah's death he lost interest in racing his horses.

After Susannah's passing, all the young girls in town witnessed the grieving widower and sought his attention, including the Lane's daughter. Ben had known Elizabeth Jane for years. Betsy, as everyone called her, was three years younger than Ben. After a year or so of feeling sorry for himself, he started to take notice of Betsy. It all started at one of the town gatherings when some of the young men began to bother Betsy. Young men often make a nuisance of themselves around pretty girls. Ben noticed that she was not enjoying the attention she was receiving and he went to her rescue.

"Betsy, would you like to get some fresh air?" Ben asked.

"Yes, --- I would like that very much." She responded.

They walked down to the creek to enjoy the full moon reflecting over the water. They sat down on a bench placed there years before for young lovers to enjoy the view in the moonlight. No one knew who placed the bench there, but all the young lovers were glad they did! Conversation started slowly and it was Betsy who finally broke the silence.

"Ben thanks for coming to my rescue tonight. If the night continued like it was going, I'm afraid I would have been miserable."

"You're quite welcome, but I can understand their attraction to you. You are the most beautiful girl there."

"Well thank you again, I didn't think you noticed." Betsy said as she stood up. She walked closer to the bank and stood there with her hands clasped behind her back twisting back and forth, making a swishing sound with the petty-coats under her long blue dress.

Ben got to his feet, walked over to her and said, "I noticed, oh, I noticed alright and standing here in the moonlight, you are even more beautiful."

"Why Benjamin Mace, you do make me blush! Are you getting fresh with me?"

"I suppose that I might be, but my intentions are honorable."

There was another lull in the conversation for a moment and then Betsy spoke, "Ben" and another pause.

"Yes Betsy, --- what do you want?"

She stood there for a moment, "Ben, you can kiss me now --- if you want too."

"I do, I want to very much." This magical night was sealed with their first kiss.

"Ben, you can do that again if you like." Ben liked it very much and many more kisses followed.

Susannah's vision of him falling in love had come to pass. Ben knew that The Creator had brought Betsy into his life to be his companion and wife. After Susannah's death Ben had no notions of getting remarried, but God's plan was much better than his own. Ben and Betsy's courtship progressed quickly after their first kiss on the banks of that creek and they were married May 1, 1854. On January 5, 1855, their first child was born. Don Pedro became his father's pride and joy. Ben was twenty-six years old and Betsy was twenty-three.

WAR APPROACHES
The Civil War

In the years before the Revolutionary War, the Cherokees had supported the English and because of their treatment during *The Trail of Tears*, no love was lost on the federal government. As the southern states sought help for their cause the Cherokees were asked for their support and a war was sure to come. By 1860 Ben and Betsy had a son five years old, a daughter, Narcissus Jane, and twins, son Robert Henry and daughter Catherine Alice. Ben was not eager to leave his family and get involved in this war. Ben shared his father's opinion that a man should not own another man and didn't want to support the south and slavery. Ben basically wanted to be left alone and let the war go on without him.

The war came closer as troops began to cross his land. His first encounter was with a band of Confederates. A young officer approached the Bob's house and called out.

"Could you provide my men with some water?" he asked.

Ben picked up his rifle, which was normal when a strange approached, and walked out to the porch. "You are welcome to draw water from the well and rest for awhile."

"Thank you, sir." As he motion to his men it was okay to get water and relax for a spell.

"Are your men hungry? We don't have much to offer, but we do have some hot biscuits and coffee." Ben replied.

"What ever you can spare would be greatly appreciated." The young officer replied.

"Betsy, can you bring out some biscuits and coffee for

these men?"

She quickly prepared more biscuits and coffee and took the food outside. As each man received food and drink, she got their thanks and after a couple of hours they cleaned up the area and continued on their way.

Both Confederate and Union forces crossed over his farm from time to time and on occasion stopping to rest and water their horses. Ben was hospitable to both sides and really did not mind their visits until a visit by group of Union soldiers. Early one morning about sunrise a ragged soldier broke into Ben's house while the family was still asleep. Before Ben could get out of bed and get his knife, the man with three stripes on his sleeve stormed into the room with another man. 'Three Strips' pulled Betsy out of bed and ripped the top of her nightgown, exposing her breasts and began rubbing them. Ben was burning with anger and had the other man not had a gun to his head, 'Three Strips' would be dead. 'Three Strips' then demanded Betsy to make breakfast for his men. She did as he commanded as Ben was held at gunpoint and the kids looked on in fear. Betsy would have gladly prepared food for the men if only asked. Their actions were not necessary. After 'Three Strips' and his men had been feed, 'Three Strips' looked around the house for anything of value to take. Nothing caught his fancy. 'Three Strips' took Ben and Betsy out side, as they were going out the door, Don Pedro only six years old hit 'Three Strips' in the back with a chair. Even at his young age, he was ready to defend his mama and papa. 'Three Strips' turned and hit him in the head with the butt of his pistol, putting a deep cut in his head. Once outside 'Three Strips' saw Ben's black stallion in the corral.

'Three Strips' instructed one of his men, "Take the saddle off my horse and put it on that stallion."

Ben said, "I don't think taking my horse is a very good idea."

"What do mean your horse? That's my horse now!" 'Three Strips' replied. "Okay men mount up, it's time to move on. So long Injun, when I come back through we'll talk about it….. and have better grub the next time."

With that 'Three Strips' and his ten men rode off to the southeast.

Ben watched as they rode out of site. He checked on Don Pedro and told Betsy he would be okay.

Ben said, "I'm goin' huntin'" He ran to the barn and grabbed two rifles, his knife and hatchet that he had hidden there for just an occasion such as this. With his rifle in his hand, he mumbled to himself, *have better grub next time! There won't be a next time white-man.* Ben had never felt hatred and rage like this before as he flung his leg across another horse, not taking time for a saddle. He was riding into battle the way his forefathers had, bareback. Ben rode through the woods in reckless abandon. In about twenty minutes, he was in position ahead of the troops and waited for them to come around the bend of the trail. His first shot rang out and knocked 'Three Strips' off the horse with a round in the chest. Before he hit the ground, another shot struck another soldier. In a flash Ben's knife was buried in the chest of his third victim. The remaining eight looked around trying figure where the shots were coming from. The echo in the woods made it difficult to determine the direction of fire. Ben could tell they were afraid and confused and took pity on them.

"Dismount and through down your weapons." Ben demanded.

They didn't know Ben was down to his hatchet as his only weapon, but they did so without hesitation. Ben came out of his hiding place and told one of the men to tie the others up. "Make sure those ropes tight, your life depends on it." Ben said. The soldier was moving as fast as he could as Ben checked after each man was bound.

"Good work young man!" Then Ben placed ropes on him, put the three dead men across the horses and gathered the weapons. Ben mounted his black stallion and said, "I think you know the direction of town, get movin'"

They started toward town with Ben and the horses close behind. Ben placed them in a makeshift jail to hold them 'til a Confederate group came through about two weeks later.

Ben's desire to remain neutral in this war was no longer possible. This action so infuriated him that he decided in favor of the Confederacy.

One of the chiefs that signed the Treaty of New Echota, Stand Watie, was asked to organize a regiment to corporate with the Confederacy. On July 12, 1861 Stand Watie formed the Cherokee Mounted Rifle Regiment and in the months ahead the First and Second Mounted Volunteers were also formed. Because of Ben's family's long friendship with Chief John Ross, Ben felt he could not join the Cherokee Regiment formed by Watie, being an old adversary of John Ross, and instead joined a company of volunteer cavalry in Little Rock formed by Thomas James Churchill. In 1861, Churchill led this unit in the state militia's expedition to seize the federal arsenal at Fort Smith. Upon Arkansas' formal secession from the Union in May 1861, Churchill recruited and was elected the Colonel of the First Arkansas Mounted Rifles. Churchill led this regiment at the battles of Wilson's Creek and Pea Ridge. Churchill was commissioned as a Brigadier General on March 4, 1862. After fighting at Richmond, Kentucky under General Kirby Smith, General Churchill completed a fortification at Arkansas Post called Fort Hindman by the end of 1862.

In the last week of December 1862, Ben led a group of Confederate forces operating out of the Post and attacked and captured the Union steamer, Blue Wing, at Cypress Bend on the Mississippi, near the town of Napoleon. The Blue Wing was headed for the Federal fleet downriver at Vicksburg. The Blue Wing was carrying supplies of ammunition and towing two barges of coal. Ben and the victorious Rebels towed the ship and its supplies up the Arkansas River to the recently completed Fort Hindman. This Confederate triumph would turn out to be the beginning of the end for Fort Hindman.

During the winter of 1862-63, Union General John McClernand was assembling for the attack on Vicksburg. Upon hearing the news of the Confederate victory, he diverted a portion of the troops under his command to attack Fort Hindman. On Friday evening of January 9, sixty steamers unloaded 32,000 Union soldiers to attack the fort from the north. On Saturday the Confederate forces were driven back to their last line of defense adjacent to the fort. Union gunboats steamed upriver and began pounding the fort on the south. On Sunday the fighting was intense, small arms fire and cannon balls cracked and boomed up and down the weakening Confederate defense line. The Union gunboats knocked out the fort's heavy artillery. Ben's unit was one of the heaviest hit. They took a beating from the artillery as well as small arms fire. Late in the battle, Ben took a musket round to his right side. Loss of blood and the pain caused him to pass out. While he was unconscious he saw his mother, wife, and son looking down into a grave. Ben was sure he was going to die or was already dead.

Overwhelmed by the strength of the Union forces, the Confederates raised white flags after a 30-hour siege. No one was more surprised by the white flags than General Churchill. He was the only one that had the authority to order surrender. And surrender was not his plan even though he realized that holding on to Fort Hindman was impossible given the enemy's superiority in men and firepower. However, he hoped to hang on until nightfall, at that time he planned to cut his way through the Union lines to safety. The appearance of the white flags made his plan impossible. General Churchill and the remainder of the Confederate command, numbering 4,793 men were taken prisoner. Many of the men were badly injured, Ben included. His survival did not look good at this time. In addition to the troops, the Union forces regained control of the Blue Wing Steamer and its cargo of small arms, black gun powder artillery rounds, small arms ammunition and draft animals. By the next day the battle was over. Although Union losses were high and the victory did not contribute to the capture of Vicksburg, it did eliminate one more impediment to Union shipping on the Mississippi.

The Blue Wing Steamer took the Rebel prisoners to the Commissioner of Exchange in St. Louis. Ben remained in a comma during the trip on the boat he had captured just a few days before. There Ben and the other injured were cared for. When Ben woke up for the first time after his injury, he found himself in a Yankee hospital. He didn't like being a prisoner very much, but he was glad to be alive. His care was not the best, but enough to keep him alive, Ben's will to live and see his family helped him endure the pain and his injuries. After several months in the hospital, Ben was released and sent to a prison camp where he remained until the war's end. His family heard of the Confederates defeat at Fort Hindman, but nothing about Ben's fate. Detailed records from the fort were not kept. A complete roster of the men stationed there was unknown. The Federal troops didn't know the names of the prisoners from the fort, much less the wounded or dead. Was Ben alive or had he perished during the battle? His family could only hope and pray that he survived.

For Ben the war was over. However, battles continued for two more years. The Union moved toward victory during the first four months of 1865 and in mid January, the capture of Fort Fisher, which guarded Wilmington, North Carolina, closed the final significant Confederate port. By May all the Confederate forces were defeated. Ironically the last General to surrender was the Cherokee commander, Stand Watie.

Early in July of 1865, as Don Pedro was tending crops in a field near the house he spotted a man walking slowly down the road toward their house. They didn't get many visitors during the week, so he stopped working, picked up a rifle and walked toward the man. As the two got closer, he recognized the man was his papa. Don Pedro dropped the rifle and rushed to his papa and helped him to the house. The entire family had given up hope that Ben was still alive until this wonderful day of reunion. Ben was told his father had past away on Sunday January 11, 1863. That was the day Ben had been shot. His vision of his family looking down into the grave was the burial of his father, not himself as he had imagined. Ben's mother was still grieving Bob's death and in very poor health herself. She died November 16, 1866 during a cold and bitter winter.

The loss of his grandmother was very difficult for Don Pedro. He had been very close to her while his father was away fighting in the war. At ten years old, despite developing some bad habits during his father's absence, he felt responsible for the family. No one was happier than he to see his father's return and assume the leadership of the family. July of 1865 was a very goodtime for Ben's family. Ben was home and through with the war. Their joy was experience by many other families as their loved ones returned home after a bitter war.

Even though Don Pedro's mother was English, he felt he was Cherokee and wanted to hold on to the Cherokee traditions. At twelve years of age he was prepared to survive in the wilderness for weeks with only his rifle, knife, and hatchet. He was only six when Ben left for the war and he had to learn much on his own. He was happy to have his papa back. Don Pedro asked his papa questions almost daily about the Cherokee traditions and legends. He wanted to learn all he could and to be a kid again.

Reconstruction was difficult after the war. Carpetbaggers and scalawags from the north made life difficult for the people in the south. Not much was left of the beautiful farms, churches, schools, and growing settlements like Shiloh and Fayetteville. Even the smaller communities that dotted the countryside suffered during the four years of war. The settlers that tamed the land to begin with rose from those ashes and once the days of reconstruction were over, they began to reclaim and rebuild again.

Ben remained in Arkansas until his mother died in 1866. At the end of the season, after the crops had been harvested and sold, Ben asked Michael to stop by the house on Saturday afternoon for a chat.

Saturday was a wonderful day. Fall in Arkansas is a beautiful time of year. The trees start showing their colors of orange, red, and brown. All of these colors added to yellow would have made a great painting Ben thought. It was a cool crisp day as Ben was sitting on the front porch, enjoying his favorite chair when Michael approached the house.

As Michael got near to the house, Ben shouted to him, "Michael, hurry, come … join me."

"Yes sir. Mr. Mace, I is movin' as fast as I can."

"Michael, please sit and visit with me awhile. Can I get you somethin' to drink?"

"Yes sir, Mr. Mace, a cool drink of water would be mighty fine after the walk over here."

Ben stood and walked over to the well and drew a bucket of water. The well was fed by an underground spring and its waters were always cool and refreshing. He returned to the porch and filled a tin-cup with water dipped from the bucket with a dried gourd. He handed the cup to Michael and then refilled his own cup. "Michael, how long have we known each other?

"I believes you be a year old when I came to work for your father."

"One year old, and to this day you call me Mr. Mace. I think it's time you started callin' me Ben."

"No sir, I don't think that be possible. You been Mr. Mace

all these years and you always be Mr. Mace. No sir, that just ain't possible."

Ben let out a tiny laugh in amusement, "Michael you have always brought laughter and happiness to me. How old were you then?"

"Oh, don't really know. I guess about twenty-five, --- maybe. Already had two boys myself. They be 'bout you age, a little older I suppose. Don't know for sure, twenty-five sounds 'bout right to me."

"That was over thirty-six years ago. That would make you sixty-one now, right."

"Don't rightly know, sometimes I feels a lot older. I got one foot here and one in glory."

"Well, that brings me to what I wanted to talk to you about. Look at all this." as Ben motioned to the farm before their eyes. "I'm thinking about movin' my family to Texas. I hear there is good farmland in northeast Texas."

"Mr. Mace, why do you want to do that? I don't think I is up to movin' again!"

"Michael, you have been a friend for many years. Your boys and I grew up side-by-side, workin' and playin' together. My father trusted you with everything he had. That included me and my family when you brought us to Arkansas when I was very young. I saw you work as hard … or harder than anyone building this farm and the life we enjoy today. To my father, you were always a free man. Now that the war is over, you are officially a free man. I have no hold on you, other than the bond we share as friends. I'm not expectin' you to uproot your family and come with us. I want to sell you this farm."

Michael sat listening to Ben's every word very carefully, "Mr. Mace, you knows I ain't got no money. How can I buy this farm?"

Ben thought for a moment, "Betsy and I have talked about this and we feel that over the years your work has been a big payment toward the purchase. I don't want to say I'm givin' the farm to you. Somehow, that makes me appear more generous than I am. We expect no payment now for the farm. But, each year after the crops have been sold, take out the cost of that year and what will be necessary for next year's crops. If you make any money, send half of it to us. That's the only payment we expect. If you make no money, you owe us nothin'."

"I is at a loss for the right words to say. Why you be so kind to me?"

"I'm not being kind at all … it's what you deserve; you've earned everythin' because of your loyal service. Do we have a deal?"

"You be very kind to this old man, yes sir, we have a deal Mr. Mace."

"Now that we are kinda like partners, can you call me Ben?"

"No sir, that ain't changed. You still be Mr. Mace."

The two stood and shook hands to seal the deal. As their hands separated, Ben pulled Michael close to himself and further sealed the deal with hug of friendship. A beautiful fall day came to an end and this phase of Ben's life in Arkansas was coming to a close.

FARMING NEW LANDS

Legend of the Strawberry

They finalized the deal during the early days of December of 1866. Ben was eager to get started even though winter approached. Ben the stories his father's told of his journey from Tennessee with the tribe taught Ben that winter could be treacherous. But he was eager to find a place to settle before the spring planting season. The second week of the month and all their possessions loaded onto the wagons Ben and his family headed for Texas. He didn't want to spend more than three weeks traveling. He had hopes of building a temporary cabin before the chill of winter set in.

Michael and his family came to wish them luck on the trip and in finding a new home. Ben and Betsy began the journey south with their six children, Don Pedro was eleven years old, Narcissus Jane was eight years old, the twins, Robert and Catherine, were six, Annie four, and the baby of the family, Lucy Matilda was one year old. Their second son, John Ruffin had died shortly after his first birthday. Ben was only eleven years old when Michael brought them west at his father's request. As Ben traveled with his children now, he thought what a pain he must have been for Michael, dealing with another man's family as well as his own. Travel was slow as he and Betsy tried to keep the children together and headed in the right direction.

At the end of the first day, Don Pedro asked, "Papa, are we there yet?"

"No Don Pedro. Not even close!" Ben replied.

Ben finished setting up their camp as Betsy prepared

supper. As they were getting ready for sleep Don Pedro asked, "Papa will you tell us a story?"

"Okay, but then you have to go to sleep. --- Do you remember the jar of strawberries that your grandmother kept in the kitchen?"

Don Pedro laughed, "Yes, every time she and grandpapa had an argument, she would start eating those berries."

"Yes she did. There is a Cherokee legend about the origin of the strawberry. When the Creator had formed the first man, the Creator then made a mate for the man. Man and woman lived together for a time and were very happy. As time passed, they began to quarrel. The woman grew tired of the quarreling and left, heading for *Nundagunyi*, the sun land in the east. The man was ashamed for what he had caused and began to follow her because he loved her very much. He followed, but the woman kept heading east and never looked behind, until *Unelanunhi* the sun took pity on the man. *Unelanunhi* asked the man if he was still angry with the woman. No, was the man's reply. *Unelanunhi* asked would you like to have her back. Oh yes, the man replied, yes I want her back. So *Unelanunhi* caused a patch of the ripe huckleberries to spring up along the trail, but she continued on her way paying no mind to the huckleberries. *Unelanunhi* then placed some blackberries along her path and still she didn't notice them. *Unelanunhi* placed other berries and then some trees covered with beautiful red fruit beside the path to tempt her. Still, the woman was unmoved until she saw in front of her, a patch of large ripe strawberries, the first ever known. She stopped to eat some and as she picked them she turn her face to the west and saw the man. The memory of her husband came back to her and she could not go on. She sat down but the longer she waited the stronger the desire for her husband became. She gathered some berries and started back along the path to share them with him. When the two came together, he greeted her kindly and they went home together. The Cherokee word for strawberry is *a-ni*. The rich lands of the old Cherokee country are noted for their abundance of strawberries and other wild fruits. Today strawberries are often kept in Cherokee homes. They remind us not to argue and are a symbol of good luck."

Ben looked at Betsy and smiled. He continued talking to Don Pedro while gazing at his beautiful Betsy, "Even though your mother is English, she has eaten many strawberries during our marriage. When you meet a young woman and you get married, remember this. Never let the sun set on your anger. This is the secret to a long and happy marriage."

The other children had fallen asleep one by one during the story and now they were all sound asleep.

"You tell a good children's story, Benjamin Mace. Now, tell me one."

Ben thought for a minute, "Betsy, --- how many strawberries have you eaten? Don't answer that! Well anyway, the story I have to tell you is much too long for one night. It is about a man and his love for a beautiful English maiden that came to dwell in his land and his heart. The young maiden has hair of gold, eyes of green, and the spirit of a goddess. Good night, my fair-haired maiden! Tomorrow's sun will be coming up much before we want and tomorrow will be another long day. I love you, Betsy."

"Tomorrow will be long, but I know our journey is worth it. --- I love you too."

The next few days progressed much as the first. They got an early start each day and stopped in the afternoon in time to establish camp before nightfall. Ben believed they were making about eight miles a day or at least he hoped for that. During the fifth day they passed through a small community called Gillham. In Gillham they replenished supplies that were running low. Later that afternoon they encountered heavy rains. Up until this day conditions could not have been better. The weather was cool, the sun was bright and clear. However, the good weather proved to be a distraction for the children. The beautiful days brought out their playful nature and at times made it difficult to keep them going in the right direction.

Day six, the trail became extremely muddy from the night's rain and it was still raining. Preparing for travel during the morning rain was the highlight of the day. Things only got worse from there on. By noon they had only gone a mile, maybe a half mile more. The rain appeared to be letting up as the sun started looking at these weary travelers from behind the clouds. Things were looking better. Ben was glad that the weather was improving, but all was not good. Ben was leading the team of horses on foot and suddenly the horses came to an abrupt stop. The wagon had slipped into a huge muddy bog on the trail.

Ben walked back to the wagon to study the situation, "Betsy, --- I think we'll take a rest stop. You and the children find a dry spot and sit for a spell."

Betsy and the children had a chance to rest, but for Ben the work continued.

Betsy asked, "Can I help?"

"No, --- Thanks though. --- I'm not sure what I'm gonna' do yet!"

Betsy took the children to an area beneath some trees near the trail. With the fall leaves on the ground it wasn't dry, but at least it wasn't muddy.

After a few minutes Betsy said to Don Pedro, "Why don't you go and help your papa? He seems to have a plan in mind and maybe you can help."

"Okay mama, I will help papa." Don Pedro was certainly eager and rushed to his papa's side.

"Papa, can I help?"

"Don't know for sure son, but I think there is a way for you to help. Here's what I plan to do. First I need a strong limb to lift the wagon. You gather some smaller branches and leaves to place under the wheel when I get it out of the mud."

"Yes papa." Without hesitation Don Pedro rushed to do as his papa had asked.

Ben looked for a long straight limb. The branch he chose was an oak limb, about eight inches around and six feet long. Ben took his hatchet and trimmed the branches off the trunk and went back to the wagon. Betsy and the younger children continued to rest and watch in the comfort of their spot under the tree.

As Ben approached the wagon he noticed the pile that Don Pedro had gathered. Wanting desperately to please his papa, he asked. "Did I get enough, papa? I can get more if this is not enough."

"You have done well, son. That will be more than enough!"

Don Pedro smiled at his papa and waved to his mother,

he was very happy he was able to help and that his papa was pleased with his work, but their work was far from yet done.

"Son, I'm going to place this limb under the axle and lift the wagon, when I get it as high as I can, place the smaller braches and leaves under the wheel."

"Yes papa."

"Okay, let's do it."

Ben started to lift the wagon. The task would have been much easier with another strong man. But, Ben bent his back and strained ever muscle in his body and slowly the wagon rose out of the mud.

"Now papa?"

Ben groaned as he struggled, "Not yet son, just a little more." Ben had lifted the wagon as far as he thought possible, but he let out a loud grunt and managed to lift it a few more inches. "Do it now and quickly please!" Ben strained to keep the wagon in the air as Don Pedro rushed to get the limbs in place. "That should do it, son. Stand clear and I'll let the wagon down."

Ben looked and the wheel was out of the bog. Hopefully when they moved the wagon forward it would remain so. "Don Pedro, you have done well. Thanks. You gathered a lot of branches, let's go ahead and place the others in front of the wheel." Before the words had ventured far from Ben's mouth, Don Pedro was already at work. Ben looked at his son, smiled and thought to himself, *my son is eager to please me and he has done so!*

Don Pedro stood back from the wagon to admire their work, "How is that papa? Do we need more? I can go get more."

"No, I believe that will be fine. But, there is more to be done. Get the reigns and when I give the signal, get the horses to pull and pull hard. I'll push the wagon and maybe we can get it on more solid ground."

"Yes papa."

In a few minutes the wagon was resting on solid ground. Ben wiped the sweat from his face and went to the water barrel on the wagon. He took the gourd and dipped out some water. Before taking a drink, he offered the water to Don Pedro. "Thanks papa!"

"No, Don Pedro, thank you. You acted like a man today. I am very proud of you."

Ben shouted to his family resting under the tree, "Betsy, gather your chicks and let's get going!"

Betsy responded, "Don't you want to rest? If just for a minute."

"Not just now, my love. I want to cover as many miles today as possible. I'll rest tonight."

By the end of day six, they were about three miles north of the community of Horatio. In another two days they reached the Arkansas-Oklahoma border. Their journey took them across the southeast tip of Oklahoma for another three days. They camped on the banks of the Red River at the end of day twelve. The next day they crossed the river into Texas and a search for new farmland would begin in a few days.

Mid-morning on the sixteenth day they entered the community of Savannah. Ben went to the post office and talked to the postmaster, Andrew Jackson Titus. Mr. Titus explained that the post office was to be shut down soon and the man to see about land was G.W. Walker anyway. Mr. Walker had a store a few miles northwest of Savannah.

Ben hurried back to the wagon and they made the short trip to Walker Springs. The general store of Mr. Walker was not hard to locate. As Ben entered the store, a friendly man from behind the counter greeted him. The man was leaning on the counter reading the newspaper. As the man straightened up, Ben figured the man to be about six feet tall. He had a long thin face and had tiny glasses on the end of his nose. The man wore a white shirt and a black bow tie. There were black ruffled garters on his arms to keep his shirtsleeves up. The man introduced himself, "G.W. Walker at your service, sir. Everybody calls me Hawk! What can I do for you?" Ben was taken by the man's friendly nature.

"Yes, Mr. Walker. I'm Benjamin Mace. Please call me Ben. Mr. Titus down in Savannah told me you were the man to see about available land in the area. My family and I have been on the trail goin' on sixteen days now and we are looking for a place to settle in this area. I understand its good farmland. --- Excuse me for asking, how did you come to be called Hawk? I ask because my papa had a wonderful experience with a hawk"

The man turned his face to show his profile and pointed to his nose. "That should answer your question. Why don't we just call ourselves friends and drop the Mr., please call me Hawk. --- I never took to the farming life myself, but folks tell me this is the best farmland in the area. I've been keeping track of the owners because of rumors the post office is moving here. If it does move, most likely I will be named postmaster. It may be years before that happen, but I do keep track of people here. I know there is a half section of land available along White Oak Creek. Here I'll show you on the map."

"How much would this land cost me?" Ben asked.

"Well, --- let me see. The land was granted to the Henderson family in 1854. His wife never liked it here and Mr. Henderson stuck it out as long as he could. They left after 'bout ten years and went back east. I suppose it is considered deserted and available to anyone that will farm it. I suppose it don't cost nothin'. Don't know what kind of house is on it, but there is one and a barn too." Hawk took a map from under the counter. Hawk pointed to the map, "Okay we are right here. Here's White Oak Creek. The land is three hundred and twenty acres along White Oak Creek, between Kickapoo Creek, here and Anderson creek, here. It's about four miles due south of here. You could make it by nightfall, but if my family had been on the trail for sixteen days, I'd camp here, get some rest, and leave in the morning."

"Thanks for your help, Hawk. You are the answer to my family's prayers. Restin' a spell does sound good to me. Thanks again." Ben turned toward the door, he was anxious to tell Betsy their good fortune.

Hawk stopped Ben before he could leave, "Ben there is a good place to camp near my place. Make camp there and have supper with us, tonight."

"Hawk, you've helped a great deal already. I have a large family and a lot of mouths to feed. But, I appreciate the offer."

"Nonsense, Hilda and I have a bunch of kids ourselves. She always fixes lots of food. A few more ain't nothin'. She loves cooking for a group. Come, I'll show you where to camp. I won't take no for an answer."

Before Ben could say no, Hawk was walking out the door. He got on his horse and said, "Come on Ben --- we're burnin' daylight. Get in your wagon and follow me."

Ben did as he was told and Betsy asked, "Ben what is going on? Who is that man?"

Ben responded, "That is G.W. Walker. It seems we are to dine with Mr. Walker and his wife Hilda tonight." During the short trip to Hawk's house, Ben filled Betsy in on all that he and Mr. Walker had talked about.

"Woe!" Ben said as he pulled back on the reigns and brought the team to a halt. Hawk stopped to point out his house on the left of the trail. Then they continued along the trail to a grassy area near a creek. The area appeared to be a recreation area for the kids. A rope hung from a tree near the bank for the kids to swing over the creek and drop in the cooling waters.

Hawk got off his horse and indicated this was the spot to camp. "Well --- here it is!" He didn't say much, at the time because he seemed to be more interested in Ben's horse tethered at the rear of their wagon. He gently ran his hands over the black stallion and commented, "This is the finest animal I've ever seen!"

Ben replied, "This is *Svnoyi,* that's Cherokee for Midnight. He's the best and fastest horse I know of. Years ago I became interested in breeding and horse racing. Folks 'round here ever have horse races?"

Hawk laughed, "Most folks in these parts don't even have a good riding horse let alone one as fine as this fella. But, yes sometimes some farmer might start bragging about his horse and he might get challenged to a race. I'm sure when word gets out 'bout your horse, someone will question his speed and offer a challenge."

Ben and Hawk laughed and then Ben said, "I meant to ask you about the painting back at your store."

"Oh, --- you are talking about the painting of the Indian girl. I'm as proud of that painting as you are of this horse. Her name was Annona. I guess she and her people lived here maybe a hundred years ago. The legend goes that she was so beautiful that she caused a great distraction among the young braves. She was the daughter of the Kickapoo chief and the braves fought for the right to marry her. Finally, the Chief gave his consent to a young brave for her hand. Before the marriage took place the young brave died. This happened on two more occasions, each time the brave died before the marriage. Her proposals of marriage ended after that. The news of her sadness had traveled far and wide. Then one day the young chief of another tribe heard of her story and sought her hand in marriage. My wife painted that portrait of her as she imagined what Annona might have looked like. She did capture a great beauty, didn't she? My wife is full-blood Kickapoo and has always enjoyed the old stories of her people."

Ben replied, "Your wife is Indian. I am Cherokee myself, from North Carolina. My wife, Betsy is English. My father was involved in the forced removal of our people in the Smoky Mountains to Oklahoma. I enjoy most of the old stories of my people, but the horrors of that journey are very hard to hear."

Hawk remarked, "Yes I heard a little about that and having an Indian wife it made me very angry. I imagine first hand accounts are not good. When you finish up here --- come on up to the house for supper. I'm sure Hilda will enjoy swapping stories with you."

That evening as Hawk was introducing his family, Ben looked at Hilda and what he saw was a little older Annona but still very attractive. It was clear to Ben that Hilda had painted a self-portrait. She was still very beautiful and Ben knew she was the girl in the painting. Hawk began to introduce their children and their oldest son, about Don Pedro's age said, "Come on, we can figure out each other's names later. Let's go have some fun before supper."

Hilda shouted at them as they ran out the door, "Don't go far, supper will be ready in an hour." Quickly the children were out of sight. "I think Billy, that's our oldest, is excited about having an Indian friend. We call him *Runnin' Wild!*"

After they shared supper and an evening of fellowship with their new friends, Ben and Betsy returned to their camp. The children were put to bed. Ben and Betsy shared the events of the day. They both knew their new friends would be a treasure forever.

Early the next morning Ben hitched the team to the wagon and prepared for their short trip to their new home. As they passed Hawk's house, they saw him standing on the front porch drinking his morning coffee. Hawk waved and shouted to them, "I'll be down later this morning to see if I can help."

Ben waved back and said, "Thanks, friend."

"Hawk is a good man!" Ben said as he smiled at Becky.

"Yes, he is a very good man." Betsy responded. "And his wife is very beautiful, don't you think?"

"Betsy, you should see the painting in Hawk's store that she painted. It's of a young Indian maiden. I know Hilda painted herself as the girl in the painting. And yes, she is very beautiful. But, she is still second to you."

"Thanks for the compliment; you got yourself out of that pretty smooth." Betsy responded.

As they approached the farmhouse, they knew from Hawk's description, they were at the right place. Ben opened the door and walked inside. It was dirty from years of neglect and wasn't very large, only three rooms. At least it would keep them dry and warm during the winter. He could start building a new house in the spring. Their home in Arkansas was much nicer, but Ben had seen much worse. Betsy started to come inside and Ben yelled, "Stop!"

"What's wrong Ben?"

"Oh --- nothin's wrong" as he picked her up and carried her over the threshold into her new home, even if he planned it to be a temporary one.

The woods were filled with all kinds of game to eat. Deer were plentiful as well as wild turkeys, rabbits and squirrel. They had found a new home and already had some great new friend. Life was going to be good here.

OFF TO THE RACES
Legend of Black Cat Thicket

During Ben's absence during the war, Don Pedro became accustomed to being undisciplined. Betsy tried to control his rebellious nature, but he needed the firm hand of his father. Don Pedro was ten years old when his father returned and things improved, at least somewhat. When Don Pedro was born Ben did tend to give him anything he wanted, especially after their second son died. As Don Pedro grew older, in many ways he was like his father, but he didn't possess his father's gentle nature. However, Don Pedro did develop his father's love for fast horses and trading abilities. Ben loved Don Pedro, but he was disappointed with him at times. Ben tried not to be too hard on him because he knew things were hard for him during his absence because of the war.

For his eighteenth birthday in 1873, Ben gave him a paint stallion. Don Pedro named him *Ayawasdi* or Scout. Ben's horse, *Svnoyi*, had died but sired a colt that Ben named *Uwetsi Svnoyi* or Son of Midnight. Father and son raced their stallions often and a clear winner was never established. It was a toss up as to which horse was the fastest.

For years Ben heard stories about of a Shawnee Indian chief in east Texas that boasted of having the fastest horses around. Ben asked Don Pedro if he would like to visit the chief and challenge his horse to a race.

"Yes!" was his reply. "But which horse shall we race?"

"You're the one that will be doing the riding, which do you want?"

"*Uwetsi Svnoyi* is fast, but if I am to ride --- I want to ride

Ayawasdi."

"Then *Ayawasdi* it is." Ben replied.

"When do we leave?"

Ben was amused at his son's eagerness, "Soon, my son. We will leave very soon."

The story goes that the Indian Chief was fond of skunks and wore a skunk skin hat. Thus he was called Black Cat. He came to his hunting camp before the Civil War. Some believe that he came prior to Texas becoming a state in 1845 Black Cat was a friend of President Houston of the Republic of Texas and was a leader among the Indians seeking peace with the new settlers in Texas. Black Cat established the hunting camp for his tribe of Shawnee Indians and returned often over a number of years. The camp was located on a grassy hill. The area was abundant with deer and small game. Nice clear creeks flowed across The Thicket. Large herds of buffalo also fed on the adjacent prairies with its tall-grass. Chief Black Cat gave his name to these thickets located nine miles north of Greenville on the South Sulfur River; about eighty miles west of the Mace farm. Deep thickets of mixed trees, brush and vines surrounded The Thicket. The Devil's Race Track as it was known is located in The Thicket and this is where the challenge races are held. The track is located north of a smaller thicket that sloped gently upwards. The soil is sandy clay with lots of scrub oaks, mostly post oaks, persimmons and wild grape. The area of the track is a giant salt lick and always seemed moist. The track is a little short of a half a mile in length and about fifty to a hundred steps across. It is definitely a good track for racing horses.

Chief Black Cat and his fast horses are known far and

wide. Every spring Kickapoo, Choctaw and Osage Indians come to challenge Black Cat's best horses.

On the tenth day of the third month of 1875 Ben and Don Pedro started their journey to Black Cat Thicket to offer their challenge to the Shawnee chief. This Monday morning was a little overcast, but didn't look much like rain. It was a good day for traveling. They traveled south along the Kickapoo Creek to the South Sulfur River and spent the first night on the bank of the river about five miles east of the village of Talco. By the third night, they were nearing Tira, which was about the half waypoint of their trip. They continued along the banks of the river forty miles or so to the west. The Thicket couldn't be missed. They reached The Thicket on the morning of the seventh day. It was a bright and clear Sunday morning as they entered the camp of Chief Black Cat. Black Cat came out to welcome his visitors. A small crowd already began assembling for the anticipated races.

"Welcome to my camp. I am Chief Black Cat of the Shawnee."

"Greetings Chief Black Cat. My name is Ben Mace and this is my son, Don Pedro. We are from the Cherokee people of North Carolina."

"What brings you to my camp?" the chief asked.

"We've heard of your horses and the races you have. My son wants to see how his horse, *Ayawasdi*, will do against your horses."

"Large groups come every year for this event, my horses lose some races. But, they win much more than they lose. I welcome and accept your challenge."

The chief walked slowly over to Scout and silently began to study the horse. He ran his hands over Scout's neck and up to his head. Slowly he moved down *Ayawasdi's* head to his mouth. The chief took a look at *Ayawasdi's* teeth. Then the chief spoke, "He's a fine looking animal! I like his markings. I know he will be a worthy opponent. I am eager to race him. We will race in three days."

About this same time in Denton, Texas there was a young card player by the name of Sam Bass. Sam became interested in horse racing in 1874 after he purchased a horse that became know as the Denton Mare. Sam worked for the sheriff caring for his livestock. When a new sheriff was elected, Sam left his job to exploit his mare's speed and won most of his races in north Texas. And as most people knew, his wins were not always on the up and up. On a hot day in early March of 1875 Sam and his friend, Henry Underwood, began drinking at the local saloon. They left after consuming just a little beyond their capacity. Being just a 'little' drunk they purchased some watermelons, which they attempted to slice apart. Sam dropped his melon causing a group of young blacks near by to hoot and jeer at the pair. Bass and Underwood became angry and started throwing rocks at the kids, which caused the new Sheriff Gerren to place them under arrest. Before they were locked up, they managed to escape. Sam and Henry jumped on their horses and raced out of town. Gerren swore out warrants against them and started his pursuit. This was the first in a long list of crimes for Sam Bass. Sam had heard of Chief Black Cat also and the two outlaws headed for east Texas to escape the law and to challenge Black Cat. The two rode hard and reached Black Cat's camp on Monday one day after Ben and Don Pedro had arrived.

The event had been planned for Wednesday evening. After the field was set with the addition of Sam's Denton Mare, it was agreed that each contestant would put up a thousand dollars and the winner would take all. Chief Black Cat's other guests placed wagers on the race and the winner's purse included the three thousand dollars each contestant had put up plus a portion of the side bets. The winner's prize would be about five thousand dollars. A great some of money changed hands for this race. Black Cat said this was the most money he had witnessed in his many years of racing at The Devil's Race Track.

The day of the race came and the three prepared for the race. Don Pedro and *Ayawasdi*, Sam on Denton Mare and Black Cat chose his fastest horse, *Ganohalidohi* or Hunter. As the start was signaled, these three magnificent animals bolt into action. The horses were churning up huge chunks of the moist sandy clay and filled the air with the sound of pounding hooves. As the race started Sam's Denton Mare took the early lead followed by Don Pedro's *Ayawasdi*. By the first turn *Ayawasdi* and The Denton Mare were side by side. *Ganohalidohi* was several lengths behind, a distant third. *Ayawasdi* was not a large horse and was very quick in the turns. As they came down the back straight *Ayawasdi* was increasing his lead over The Denton Mare. Around the last turn and onto the front straight, *Ayawasdi* was on his way to an easy victory. Don Pedro was basking in his soon to come victory after coming around that last turn. Then the cheating of Sam and his partner came into play. Henry stepped onto the track in front of Don Pedro causing *Ayawasdi* to stumble and fall. Don Pedro broke his arm in the fall and was unable to get remounted. Then he slapped *Ayawasdi* on his flank and *Ayawasdi* bolted for the finish line. *Ayawasdi* crossed the finish line first well ahead of Denton Mare, but without Don Pedro on his back. Don Pedro's rider-less *Ayawasdi* was disqualified and Denton Mare was declared the winner, but before Sam could collect his winnings, Underwood warned him the sheriff was headed their way. Sam and Henry jumped on their horses and escaped before collecting their winnings. Sam headed south for San Antonio and Underwood headed for New Mexico. Don Pedro and Black Cat split the winner's purse and everyone was happy, except Sam Bass of course. Sam was killed in a gunfight in Round Rock several years later. Henry Underwood's fate is unknown. One story had him changing his ways and becoming a lawman in New Mexico. Quite a different story told of his demise in the arms of a jealous man's wife. Judging from his past character the last story seemed more likely.

Ben and Don Pedro returned home with the satisfaction that they had the fastest horse in Texas. Since they never determined which horse was faster, *Ayawasdi* or *Uwetsi Svnoyi*, they had the two fastest horses in Texas.

DON PEDRO MACE

Later Days

Don Pedro was very protective of his younger sister, Narcissus Jane. Norrie was a very attractive young woman of eighteen years and had many gentleman callers. Don Pedro felt compelled as her older brother to approve of each of her suitors. He very rarely approved and if he had his way, Norrie would become an old maid. Don Pedro was on the wild side himself and probably judged her suitors by his own character. No one would be good enough for his little sister. Norrie didn't approve of his life style and felt he was in no position to judge her suitors. This resulted in friction in their relationship for years.

In 1878 Norrie got to give her opinion of Don Pedro's new friend. Margaret Annie Jones had finally gotten Don Pedro's attention after all the years they had known each other. Annie was eight years younger than Don Pedro, but he had known her from town gatherings for many years. She was only fifteen, but was already attracting the eye of the young men in the area. Lucky for Don Pedro, Norrie liked Annie and thought she could be the one to put Don Pedro on the right path. She approved of his courtship of Annie. As Annie and Don Pedro courted, his behavior improved greatly. He settled down and stopped drinking. Norrie and their father were please with the new Don Pedro. Annie and Don Pedro tied the knot on October 9, 1879; just twenty-one days shy of Annie's sixteenth birthday. Don Pedro was twenty-four.

Married life seemed to agree with Don Pedro, but for only a short time. Working all day long in the fields and falling into bed exhausted each night, left him with the desire for those wild days before he married Annie. He had a wandering eye for pretty women and a weakness for drinking. These two problems would be his down fall. Even though he liked beautiful women, he was never unfaithful to Annie. He enjoyed flirting and drinking with the loose women of the area, but never to the point of betraying his marriage vows. The drinking was another issue. Annie had no tolerance for his drinking and it continued to be a problem between them. When Don Pedro was drunk, he was ill tempered and often got into fights. However, he was never abusive to Annie.

After two years of their troubled relationship, Annie became pregnant. She was excited and hoped that a child might change Don Pedro for good. She gave birth to their first child July 27, 1882. This child seemed to be the answer to their problems. Their son, Newton, turned Don Pedro into the man Annie hoped he would be. This too was to be short lived. Newton died before his sixth birthday. His death brought great pain to Don Pedro and he fell back to his drinking. Annie mourned the loss of Newton also and had no one of strength to lean on. She endured the loss of Newton alone and became very bitter. Don Pedro became more ornery, profane and tough, but when sober he was generous, loving, and respectful. He was a teller of tall tales and an insatiable perpetrator of practical jokes. The word 'bored' wasn't a part of his vocabulary.

Robert Henry, named after his grandfather, was born February 15, 1883. July 17, 1884 Lucy was born followed by Georgia August 3, 1887. Penelope 'Nellie' Elizabeth was born March 26, 1892. Don Pedro delighted in each of his children and was a good provider for his family. Despite his care and devotion to his family, he was never able to overcome his drinking problem.

After one of Don Pedro's drinking sprees in early May of 1893, he came home badly beaten. He couldn't or wouldn't tell who had beaten him. The truth of the matter was he was so drunk, he didn't know who beat him. Suffering from internal injuries, his condition worsened and on the eighteenth day of May, he past away leaving Annie with four children and expecting another. Annie gave birth to their last daughter, Donnie Pedro, on January 18, 1894, eight months to the day after Don Pedro's death. Nellie was just a year old when her father died so she only knew him from the stories she heard from older family members and their friends. Nellie's mother, Annie, married Robert Blanton Uzel on July 10, 1898 and this was the only father that Nellie was to know. Nellie was 1/4 Cherokee and with the loss of Don Pedro much of the Cherokee traditions and stories were lost to her and the family. The old stories were no longer being told and were gone with his passing.

THE KING CLAN

COMING TO AMERICA

Backtracking a bit to trace the King family's moves across the southern United States to Red River County in Texas. Both the Mace and King families had their beginnings in North Carolina. In the early 1800's they lived within one hundred miles of each other. Being Cherokee, the Mace family, except Bob, moved to Arkansas before the forced removal of the tribes in North Carolina and Tennessee. The move saved them from life on the reservation; instead they continued their good life in Mena, Arkansas and later to their Red River home in east Texas. The King's moves were voluntary and only to achieve a better life for their families.

The Abigail sailed from Dublin, Ireland with a cargo of dissident troublemakers headed for the new world. William King was aboard and a member of that group. Although he was a rebellious young man, he never landed in serious trouble, but enough trouble to be shipped to America. Over several generations the King family settled in Sampson County, North Carolina. A descendent of William King named William Wiley King having no particular skills, sought employment where he could find it. As a young man of twenty-three years, he was strong and able. He had his fill with the wrong side of the law and vowed to be a better man than his name sake. His first year was spent as a dockworker in Wilmington, a shop clerk in Clinton, and finally a farm worker in the Clinton area. William discovered he was suited for farming and it was honest work. It was hard work, but he had no problem with hard work. William worked for five years before saving enough money to purchase a farm of his own about 10 miles southwest of Clinton in the community of McDaniels. It had a large Irish population and was founded by an Irishman. In 1810 William started farming for himself. His primary crops were cotton and tomatoes. Just barely making a living from year to year, he continued to work hard and buy more land. By 1815, he had acquired two hundred acres. Although not a rich man, he made a good living.

The same year he bought his farm, William met Sarah Goldwin at a town social. The Goldwin family was new to the area and immediately William was quite taken by their daughter. Sarah was an eighteen year old beauty and William was ten years her senior. She was a small woman, but was well developed for her age. Her dark brown hair was long, almost to her waist. Her eyes were the darkest brown that William had ever seen. William was amazed at her beauty and her charm. Every young man in the area had designs on her including William. William was not tall himself and somewhat weathered by a life out doors. Despite his ruff exterior, Sarah found him attractive. Although William had not established himself as a successful farmer, Sarah decided to accept his advances to her. William was in love for the first time in his life. They courted for a short time and were married September 14, 1808.

William's farm grew and his family also, John was born in 1809. Another son, Henry was born a year later. Both boys were born at home and delivered by a local midwife. William and his sons spent a lot of time together. By the time the boys were ten and eleven they had been taught to shoot, hunt, and fish. Hunting and fishing were very important to the early pioneer families. Their catch added much needed food to the table.

William and Sarah had a good life and enjoyed each other's company very much. He was particularly proud of her and enjoyed showing everyone how much he loved her. He planned a party for their tenth wedding anniversary with the help of the town's people. He possessed some musical talent and played the fiddle at the town gatherings. It was his delight to share the folk music his family brought from Ireland. At the party, he and his band played their Irish tunes as the town people danced, ate and partied. One by one members of the band took breaks to dance with their wives or girl friends as the others in the band played on. Near the end of the evening, William called Sarah to the stage and sat her in an old wooded rocker.

Sarah looked around and looked at several different people, trying to get a clue as to what was going on. If anyone knew, they didn't let on. William knelt in front of her and proclaimed, "Sarah, happy anniversary! This last song is for you." William rosined up the bow and took his fiddle and began to play. As the band played a soft and slow Irish tune, William started singing his love song to her,

"When first I saw the Love light in your eyes
The world held nothin' but joy for me
My only dreams are dreams of you

Come live in my heart, and pay no rent
Sarah, my one true love

I love you as I never loved before
When first I saw you on the village green
Come to me and join your dream with mine

I love you as I never loved before

Come live in my heart, and pay no rent
Sarah, my one true love

When your wedding ring was new
Dreams that we dreamed came true
I remember with pride
That day we stood side by side
The beautiful picture
You made as my bride

Come live in my heart, and pay no rent
Sarah, my one true love

Love's refrain remains
The day you changed your name
When your wedding ring was new

Come live in my heart, and pay no rent
Sarah, my one true love"

By the end of the song, not a dry eye was to be found in the village. As the band continued to play, William took her in his arms embrace and they shared the final dance of the evening as everyone looked on. It was quite obvious that they remained in love as much as ever.

Years later, when Henry was twelve, he asked his father, "Papa, why did your family leave Ireland and come to America?" No one had ever asked that question before. Sarah was curious, but she never asked. Henry was not like his mother. He was very curious and wanted to know everything. William was comfortable with no one knowing his family's checkered past, but he wasn't trying to hide it. "I was a bit of a trouble maker in my early manhood and a lot like the first of my family to reach these shores. My family was very poor and when his parents died he was left alone at the young age of eighteen. He was in and out of trouble for the next five years. His biggest crimes were of survival, stealing food and trespassing just trying to get a good night sleep. He was arrested for vagrancy and theft. He was given two options, go to jail or go to America. He didn't know much about America, but he did know about jail and knew he didn't like it. So, he choose not to go to jail again and he came to America in the 1600's. This is the story that has been passed down for generations. I was a lot like him getting' in trouble all the time. However, I've made a lot of changes in my life and life here has been good since. Your mother is my greatest joy and having two fine boys are my greatest accomplishment."

William's boys were typical brothers. Henry and his older brother were constantly fighting and arguing. But, if anyone else said or did something to either, they had the other to contend with.

In 1831, young Henry took a bride. He was twenty-one and Hanna Abrams was only sixteen. After they were married, the young couple moved Merry Hill near the Albemarle Sound on the east coast of North Carolina. The area is known as Sir

Walter Raleigh's Lost Colony. Henry and Hanna also had two sons, John Elvin was born in 1832 and William Smith was born in 1834. William was named after his grandfather, but every one called him Billy. Billy's delivery was very difficult and his birth left Hanna unable to bear any other children. Hanna's health remained a problem. As Billy grew older, he took care of his mother while his older brother and dad worked the fields.

Caring for his mother was Billy's only desire. By the time he was ten, he developed an interest in medicine. During the monthly trips to the family home by the doctor to check on Hanna's condition, Billy constantly asked the doctor questions. During his high school days he worked for the doctor after school and on the weekends doing odd jobs and continued to ask questions.

Billy graduated from high school when he was seventeen. He had found favor with the doctor and with his help, enrolled at the college at Raleigh and attended medical school after that. During medial school Billy met Sarah Ann Jones. They were married and had a daughter, Frances Jane by 1856. In 1859 Billy received his medical degree. After graduating Dr. King relocated his young bride and daughter to Winnfield, Louisiana. Another daughter, Lydia Ann was born in 1861 and in 1864 their son, Seneca Jones was born.

Things were difficult for Billy and his family during the Civil War and the reconstruction after the war was even more difficult. Billy decided to move his family to Texas. He made the arrangements for his family's relocation to northeast Texas, near the Red River. However, Billy had a patient at the time expecting her first child. The young girl was unmarried and Billy stayed behind for her child was born. Billy hired a man to take his wife and children to Texas without him.

In the summer of 1870 Sarah and her three children settled in rich farmland adjacent to the Mace farm. They moved into an established farmhouse and started their new life near Kickapoo Creek. Things were difficult with Bill. The children started school and began to settle into the new area. Young Seneca was in the first grade and missed his father. One afternoon he came home from school and found his mother was crying. She was holding a letter in her hand.

"Mama, why are you crying?" he asked.

My Dear Sarah,

I'm sorry that this letter will not bring good news to you or happiness either. My patient here had complications with the birth of her child. The truth of the matter is, it is my child. It is with great sadness that I tell you this. She is not nearly as strong as you and I have decided to remain here and start a new life with her and the son she bore.

Please forgive me!

Billy

She couldn't find the right words to tell him that his father wasn't coming. She just said he was delayed. Sarah struggled to support her family without help from her husband. Despite not having their father to influence their upbringing, the children developed into good honest adults with the strong influence of Sarah. Sarah never spoke a bad word about Billy.

Only she knew what her heart felt about the situation.

Seneca worked as a farm hand very early in life to help support his mother and his older sisters. He worked very hard to purchase his own farm just as his great grandfather had done after arriving in America. Seneca's father was the only King that had taken a different career choice and became a doctor. The rest of the family remained farmers. It would appear that his father also failed to inherit the strong sense of family and the capacity for hard work as the rest of the family.

Seneca purchased a few acres from the Ben Wheelus family. He had done work for Mr. Wheelus and he was impressed with young Seneca's hard work ethic. Seneca was only twenty years old and managed to make a fresh start for his life. During this time he began to court Ben's daughter. In 1884, Seneca and Henrietta Josephine Wheelus were married. Both were twenty-one years old. They started their family with a daughter in 1885. Her name was Eula Colestra. Iley Joel was born November 8, 1886. Lula Bell was born two years latter and died before her first birthday. Another son, Hiram Burris, was born July 30, 1890. Life was difficult and often short in the late 1800s, as Seneca's family would realize. Another daughter died before her third birthday. The boys seemed to make it to adulthood just fine. William Wiley was born February 14, 1894. Another daughter, Oma Fay, died less than two months after her birth. Their last child, Martin Newell, was born December 1, 1897. Of their eight children, only five lived to be adults. The only daughter to survive was their first child, Eula.

NELLIE ELIZABETH MACE
Mamma Nell

The turn of the century brought many changes. The horse had been the mainstay of American existence since the first settlers arrived in the new land. Families could not survive without the aide of their horses. Their horses were used to clear the fields, prepare those fields for planting, take the crops to market and were the only means of transportation. They used their horses to travel to town for purchasing supplies. The families relied on their horse to get them to church on Sunday and when a family member became ill, the horse was ridden to summon the doctor. When the elderly past on, the horse pulled the wagon that delivered them to their final resting place. The 1900's ushered in the mechanical age and one of the greatest periods of change in world history.

Life in the late 1800's and early 1900's was a time of tremendous change in the way that people lived. A practical gasoline powered vehicle was developed in Germany and ushered in the age of the horseless carriage. By the early 1900s, gasoline cars started to out sell all other types of motor vehicles. The horse had been the backbone of American life since the nation was formed. However, the horseless carriage days were here to stay. This changed the way people traveled and the way they worked, making life much easier.

Electrical lighting systems were being installed in the finer home during the early 1900s and with time made available to the farm communities as well. The first successful airplane made its flight on December 17, 1903. The mechanical age developed at a rapid pace during the first part of the century.

Suddenly the dreams of men became reality. Despite what was happening in the big cities of the world and improvements made to everyday life there, life on the farm was slow to change. Nellie, her brothers, and sisters roamed the area around their farm barefoot in the warm days of spring. They amused themselves as kids had done for years. They sampled the taste of honey from the honeysuckle blooms and enjoyed the smell of the smokehouse in the spring when its aroma filled the air. Nellie's brothers fished in the creeks while Nellie and her sisters picked wild flowers. Getting bellyaches from eating too many green apples, climbing trees, and swinging on a grapevine for a splash in the creek were all part of their youth. The loft of the barn was a magical place and provided a playground for the young ones.

Nellie learned to cook at her mother's apron as did her sisters. Their mother was a wonderful cook and taught her girls her many secrets of cooking. Every day before the sun came up; the smell of hot biscuits filled their home. Generous portions of ham from the smokehouse and pear preserves were regulars at the breakfast table. As the young ones got older their responsibilities increased. The boys helped in planting and harvesting, while the girls gathered eggs, milked the cows, and churned butter. Crops provided income for the family as well as food for the table. Eggs and butter were sold to area families to supplement the family income and provided food for the family too.

Although Nellie didn't remember her father, her mother told her of her dad often. Her mother said Don Pedro was tall, dark and very handsome. As Nellie got older, her mother told her she looked very much like her father. She had the high cheekbones of the Cherokee Indians and their dark skin.

Most of the time girls don't like to be told they look like their fathers, but Nellie was proud of her Indian roots. Nellie was a very attractive female version of Don Pedro.

Holidays, particularly in the spring and fall provided times of gathering for the community where music, eating, dancing, and a little drinking were enjoyed. Nellie's mother and the other ladies made their best recipes for these occasions in the desire to showcase their talents. Each category of the meal was judged and awards given. Nellie's mother was a consistent winner. Nellie's mother was a very religious woman and devout Christian lady and didn't believe in dancing or drinking. Nellie and her sisters were instilled these same qualities. Even though Nellie's mother disapproved of drinking, she did enjoy the fellowship with their neighbors along with the music and eating of the events. Having folks brag on her fine meals was a reward in its self.

1906 was a bad year for farming in east Texas. There was far too much rain that made planting difficult and with the wet conditions, many crops failed. Seneca Jones King yearned for a better place for his family and decided to move them to Oklahoma. Eula, his oldest child, was twenty-one years old and married to Charles Coleman. They remained in Texas along with Iley. Iley was twenty years old and decided to remain on the family farm and endured the hardships of the wet spring. Iley's decision to stay was not so much to prove he could make a living on the land, but because of a young woman, Nellie Mace that lived near by

When Nellie was fifteen she asked her mother, "Iley has asked me for a date, can I go, please?"

"Who is Iley?" her mother responded.

"You know him, Iley Joel King. He lives on the farm next to ours."

"Yes, I do know him and he is much too old for you. Where does he want to do on this date?"

"He asked me to a birthday party for Jethro Tillman at their house. Please can I go? We'll be home early." Nellie pleaded.

"Whose house, the King's or the Tillman's?" her mother asked.

"The Tillman's, Iley's family has moved to Oklahoma. Iley is looking after their farm, but lives with his sister. She is married to Charles Coleman." Nellie replied still pleading her case.

"The Tillman's are good people. Well if it's OK with your father, you can go."

Nellie hadn't expected her mother or stepfather to allow her to go on this date and expected a very long debate. She was caught totally off guard when they said she could go, as long as her sister, Georgia Mae, went along. Her sister was five years older. At Nellie's young age she was not 'fully growed' as her family said. The date went well and Iley and Nellie had many more After the courting was done the Reverend Goode married Iley and Nellie on December 7, 1907. Just six months after Nellie's fifteenth birthday, their first child, Berris, was born on September 5, 1908 and was their only daughter. As a few years went by, Nellie and Iley became a bit of a mismatch. Nellie became 'fully growed' and grew taller. Iley was not a large man in stature and she stood a head taller than him. Six brothers followed Berris. Dan was born March 18, 1910. S.J. followed August 2, 1912 named for his grandfather, Seneca

Jones King. William was born on September 5, 1914 followed by my dad, Henry Lane on November 5, 1916. I assume the name 'Lane' came from Don Pedro's mother's maiden name. Everyone called him 'Buck'. Almost five years later Rudolph was born on September 2, 1921. Nellie and Iley's last son was born on July 3, 1928. Robert Blanton was the baby of the family. Twenty years separated R.B. and his oldest sibling, Berris.

Jay was a sort of hobo or more of a free spirit that roamed the area. He worked when he could or when he wanted, but he wasn't ambitious or hard working, just a drifter. He was harmless and all the men liked him. He had wild stories to tell and the men enjoyed hearing them. The truth of his stories were always suspect, but he could spin a good yarn. If he came by and no one was around, he calmly fixed himself a meal, clean up afterwards and leave. He never did any harm, but the women didn't like him and were concerned he might cause trouble. One day Nellie caught him in her garden. Nellie was as gentle as the flowers she grew and loved, but just as tough as the situation called for. Her garden was her private domain and even Iley didn't invade its privacy. She met Jay with Iley's shotgun and told him to get out of her garden. Jay never moved with a great deal of speed and he didn't respond as quickly as Nellie thought he should. She fired a shot into the ground at his feet. "If you keep diggin' in my garden, dig it deep, cause that's where your gonna be buried."

Jay did a little dance and said, "Nell, what are you doing. I'm just getting' a little food. You ain't gonna miss it. You know you ain't gonna shot me."

Nellie responded, "Jay, what part of 'get out of my garden'

do you no not understand!" And she fired another shot a little closer to his feet.

Jay rethought his position, "OK Nell, I'm leavin' before you reload." He left quickly and never to return to her garden.

Nellie milked her two cows every day. She churned butter and made cheese, buttermilk and cottage cheese, things she learned at her mother's side. Nellie was well known for her cottage cheese. She always knew when the curds were just right. The curds were put in cheesecloth and salted, then mixed with pure cream. It was difficult for her to get things done because of the constant interruptions of people coming by to purchase her goods. Nellie was a very quite lady and was unable to explain her problem to her customers. It grew so bad that finally she did tell one of her close friends and the word got out. Her customers started coming on Sunday afternoon to make their purchases. Nellie didn't like to conduct business on the Sabbath day or as she said 'The Lord's Day', but it did give her more time to do her chores during the week.

LIFE WITH SIX BROTHERS

Berris King

Berris must have had a difficult time with six brothers. As she grew older she helped her mother with the household chores including milking the cow, gathering eggs, and churning butter. The boys worked the fields with their dad. In those days everyone pitched in to get things done and help family members. People often talk of 'the good ole days.' I think every generation considers their childhood years as 'the good ole days'. Times were hard in the late 1800s, but families were close and those were indeed 'good ole days.' Today families go this way and that way and at times don't take time to eat or spend time together. Both fathers and mothers work, often the children are left to take care of themselves. Because of this the family units are on the verge of extinction and we wonder why we have lost the good ole days.

Two of Berris' brothers, Bill and Buck, made violins or as country folks called them fiddles. I learned later that they also performed at school and town functions. Buck played the banjo and rode bulls at the county fair. Bill played the fiddle and was a very mysterious man. Bill and Buck had an altercation one night fighting for the family's horse to go on a date. A fight broke out and somehow Bill got stabbed in arm. Buck got the horse and went on his date. Bill stayed home and tended his wounds. Needless to say Buck didn't have a good time on his date. He was only thinking of what he had done to his brother. Their mom and dad never found out what happened that night. As a child I remember Bill coming to family gatherings and he seemed to appear from out of nowhere. Bill was deaf and spoke very softly and at times it seemed he only moved his lips. At family gatherings Berris and her brothers sat around the living room spinning stories from the past and their families. Then someone would notice that Bill had come in at sometime. However, no one could say when. His exit was just as mysterious. Although these siblings were only one-eighth Cherokee, Bill often times seemed more Cherokee than the others. Bill was a thin small man like his father and to many he was a little strange. Somewhere in northeast Texas, Bill discovered an old Indian community probably Kickapoo. He gathered pots, arrowheads, and many other Indian artifacts and displayed them in his home. His collection was quite extensive and many museums could have used his collection.

I didn't know Bill's wife, Abilene. She left Bill years before, leaving him and their children to his peculiarities. One of Bill's artifacts was a complete Indian skeleton in a cardboard box under his bed. He would take the bones out of the box and arrange them on the floor for anyone who wanted to see it. He also kept a pet skunk that he had dissented himself. The skunk kept his barn clear of rats. Many people asked him to reveal the location of his Indian find. But their questions remained unanswered. Bill took the exact location of his Indian find to his grave.

Iley or 'Daddy King' as I called him may not have been a tall man, but he was the best grandfather a boy could have. As a teenager, we stood eye to eye, but I always looked-up to him. My dad, Buck, had left the farm shortly after graduating from high school to escape the farm life and see the world. The nation was in the midst of the Great Depression. Life on the farm was not affected that much as Buck said, "We were dirt poor, but we didn't know it. We had this beautiful farm and we never went hungry." Buck joined the CCC, Civilian Conservation Corp. and for the first time in his life experienced something other than farm life.

When we returned for visits during my pre-teen years, Daddy King took me with him to run his traps and he let me shoot the animals in the traps. I know this doesn't seem sporting, however most of the animals were still alive and a trapped animal is sure to bite, the shooting was necessary. He trapped the animals for food and sold their pelts for a little extra money. Sometimes as we approached a trap, Daddy King would take the 22-rifle from my hand. "There is a skunk in this trap and you only get 1 shot at him or we might get sprayed." I could have done it, he had taught me well and I was an excellent shot for a young boy. He pulled me all around the yard when we returned home skinning the animals. It was my duty to hold the rear legs as he pulled the hide off. It seemed like the legs were going to come off in my hands and I didn't pull hard enough. "Hold on! Their legs won't come off," he told me over and over again. My mother had a red fox stole made from a fox that he had trapped and shot by me. When he took me fishing, he nearly walked me to death. We walked for a long time and finally threw our hooks into the water. If we didn't get a bite soon, we were off to the next creek. Those were wonderful times, spent with my grandfather in the woods.

As I became an adult and started my family, trips to my grandparents became less frequent. When I was forty-one, my mother died at the age of sixty-one. My dad was in very poor health when she passed away, but he was able to remain at home for about five years. His care became my responsibility and I placed him in a nursing home near my office. I wanted him near me so I could visit him often. In my dad's final days, he shared many stories that I had never heard before. The knife fight with Bill was one of those stories. My dad had trouble remembering what happened last week or even yesterday. But, he could remember the old days like they were yesterday. At times he spoke to me like he didn't know me or maybe he thought I was one of his brothers. I don't know.

As we visited in the nursing home, he revealed more to me in his last year than we had shared in the forty-seven previous ones. One particularly drizzly day he shared this story with me, "This weather reminds of when my wife found out she was pregnant with our first child, we were living in Humble, Texas. That's where my wife's family lived. When she told me the news, we decided to make a trip to my folks to tell them the news. We had no car, so we took the train to Dallas. Then we caught a bus to Annona. My dad never drove, so we had to hitchhike to their farm just north of Box Elder in the drizzling rain. Hitchhiking on the county road with my wife two months pregnant, that was a sight to behold! By the time we reached their house, we were soaking wet to the bone. After our visit we returned to Humble, just like we had come except it wasn't raining then."

I was that first child and my dad told me the story like I was a stranger. Learning these things about him was wonderful, but I had many other questions I wanted to ask, but he passed away before I got the chance. Some years later, I learned about my dad playing at town gathering from an unusual source. My new bride, Wanda, and I were going on a cruise to Alaska. As we were standing in line to board the ship, I overheard two women trying to tell two other women where Annona was located. She asked one of the ladies, "Do you know where

Paris, Texas is?"

"Yes," she replied.

The first woman continued, "Annona is about half way between Paris and New Boston."

At this point I felt compelled to interrupt, "Excuse me, I couldn't help hearing your conversation. I not only know where Annona is, but where Box Elder is as well."

Box Elder is one of those towns that if you blink, you'll miss it. Except the road ended at Box Elder and there was no place to go except back the way you came.

In amazement the first lady responded, "Are you from that area?"

"No, I'm not, but my grandfather lived on a farm about half way between Annona and Box Elder, near Crystal Lake."

"Who was your grandfather?" she replied.

"Daddy King"

"Good Lord, everybody knows Daddy King, who's your daddy?"

"I'm Buck's boy! My name is Larry and this is my wife Wanda."

"Well I do declare, Buck was a classmate of mine in school. He and his brother Bill used to play at our dances and other socials. Buck was very good looking, but was very shy. He didn't say much, but he could make beautiful music with his banjo and fiddle. There wasn't a girl in our class that didn't have a crush on Buck. He broke a lot of hearts after graduation when he joined the CCC and left home."

It's normally Wanda that runs into someone that she had

known. In fact she ran into a former co-worker on this trip. We had travel from Texas to Seattle and running into someone from Annona who knew my dad was unbelievable. I wish my dad hadn't been such a quiet and secluded man. There is much about him that will forever be a mystery and the stories lost, just as the Cherokee stories were lost to my grandmother when her father died. However, it was nice to learn this little tidbit of information from an old friend of his.

This is my saga of two families migrating west. Both families made their way west for different reasons, political and economical. Over one hundred years have passed and life today is much different. 'The Trail of Tears' was a terrible time for the Cherokee people and American history as well. The Mace family was very fortunate to escape the ordeal of life on the reservation and achieve a better life in east Texas.

I leave you with these words. There is a saying among the Indians, "We will be remembered by the tracks that we leave." There is not a word in the Cherokee language or any other tribe for "own." All Indians shared the land and all that was in it. There were conflicts to be sure over land among the Indians, but they had no concept of owning the land. Yet, the land they did not own was taken from them and each tribe was pushed into small reservations, never to regain their glory years before "The Trails of Tears" because of the greed of the early settlers and the government.

SON OF FIRE DESCENDENTS

The children of Mamma Nell and Daddy King had many children of their own, grandkids as well. To list those would be beyond my knowledge of the family, but this is Henry "Buck" Lane King's family. Everyone in the family called him Uncle Buck, but he wasn't like the Uncle Buck in the movie with John Candy. No, he was a much different man indeed. When he struck out on his own to see the world, his world changed after arriving in Humble, Texas. It was there he met Nora Gladys Goss and later took as his bride. After serving in the CCC he worked for Exploration Survey Company until he retired. Mom and dad moved to Freeport Texas where I was born April 10, 1942. Working for an oil exploration company, we moved often. Four years later we were in Mobile, Alabama where Patricia Ann King was born October 23, 1946. Eleven years from my birth we were living in Wetaskwin, Alberta, Canada were our baby sister, Sylvia Jo King, was born on November 12, 1952. Mom had to fight the nurses at the hospital to give her the name Jo. They insisted Joe was a boy's name. However, mom argued it is Jo; without the e. Mom's favorite singer was Jo Stafford and she insisted that her baby girl's name was going to be Jo. They compromised with Sylvia Jo. This was to be the last child born to mom and dad.

We almost lost Jo while on out trip back to The States. We left Canada in the midst of what they called Indian summer, very mild and wonderful weather for late November. When we reached Montana thing were terrible different. We were driving through the Rocky Mountains with snow and ice covering everything, the heater in our Hudson was running full blast, we had our coats on and wrapped in blankets. And yet we were still so very cold. Dad stopped in a small mountain town to have the heater checked. Dad was told the heater was doing all it could and informed the temperature was 50 degrees below zero. I'm not sure which was worse, the cold or the snow and ice. I remember on one occasion skidding back and forth as our dad was fighting the steering wheel to bring the Hudson under control and I looked out the side window. All I could see were the trees far below. We would surely have been killed if we had gone over the edge.

But, we made it out of the mountains as far as Butte. Jo was very sick with an extremely high temperature. Dad checked us into a motel and he and mom took Jo to a Catholic hospital where she stayed about two weeks. Mom and dad stayed at the hospital most of the time and we were told to stay in the room while they were away. I was 10 and Patsy 6 and I believe we attempted to be obedient, but how much time could we entertain ourselves before the allure of the snow caused us to disobey. We had read our collection of comic books several times over and were bored. We could see a hill behind our motel room and the Sisters of the hospital were sledding down the hill. Oh, the allurement of sin is always is so compelling. In our bored and weakened state, we put on our coats, gloves and caps to go "play" with the Nuns. The Nuns shared their sleds with us and we had a wonderful time that afternoon. We were not old enough to understand how serious Jo's sickness was and we were only thinking of our pleasure. But our pleasure was soon to come to an abrupt end when dad returned that evening.

"What did you kids do this afternoon"? He asked.

I was the eldest so I replied, "We stayed in the room and read our comic books.

He looked at Patsy and asked, "Patsy, is that what happened"?

"Yes daddy. That's what we did". came her response.

He shook his head slowly back and forth and walked over to the window. "Come here" he said as he pointed to the hospital on the other side of the hill, "Do you see that window, this end of the hospital on the top floor? We have a pretty good view of the slope on the other side. Today we saw the Nuns enjoying their afternoon sledding down the hill time and time again. Later in the day two kids joined them. You know they had coats just like the two of you".

We knew we had been busted and then I asked, "Daddy are you goin' to whip us"? I am sure I gave the most pitiful look that I could muster and Patsy started crying.

Daddy thought for a moment. He was a firm father, but he was a fair one as well. "No I'm not going to spank you. I understand how boring its must be in this room all day long. Sledding with the Nuns looked like a lot of fun; I almost wish I had been with you. But you sister is very sick. Your mom and I are very worried we may lose her".

I saw a look of sadness on his face I had never seen before. He knelt down and embraced us in his arms. His hug was firm and had such love that was difficult for him to display. The story has a happy ending, Jo got better and recovered from pneumonia and she became the joy of his life.

After a year in Rule, Texas we moved to Dallas and our travelling days were over. We spent a year in a trailer park on the west side of Dallas before mom and dad bought a house on the east side. Patsy, Jo and I grew up at 9535 East Lake Highlands. This small rock house was our first home that didn't have wheels under it. It has a big yard and was a great place to be a kid. One by one, we all graduated from Bryan Adams high school.

I was the first to leave the family nest. I married my high school sweetheart, Shirley Ann Kent in March of 1961 just short on my 19th birthday. Very quickly we had two wonderful kids, Larry Lane King, Jr. and Paige Ann King by the time we were twenty-one. Lane married Debra Arms and this year 2012 they celebrated their twenty-fifth wedding anniversary. Our grandson Taylor Lane King is a young man today nearing the completion of his studies at Texas University in Austin. Paige married Larry Wood after graduating college and sadly her marriage only lasted four years. I am very proud of our kids and grandson. They all are doing well in life and serving our Savior in many different ways. How could a father not be proud? Sadly I lost Shirley to cancer in 1996. But God wasn't through with me. He sent another beautiful lady to be my bride in 1998. To be blessed with two wonderful women, two great children and a terrific grandson is more than I deserve. God is so good!

Patsy was the next to be wed. Shortly before her graduation from BA, she married J.C. May. They have four children, Dana, Christopher, Angie and Jessica. Dana has 3 boys, Michael, Tony, and Josh. Christopher has 3 children, Brianna, Bailey and Johnathon. Brianna has a baby, Brooklynn. Angie has 3 daughters, Lacey, Amanda and Megan. Lacey has a baby, Orion. Jessica has 2 sons, Clayton and Cameron. Patsy and J.C. divorced and later she married Ray Massey. I always liked J.C. a lot, but he wasn't good to Patsy. Ray is another story. He is very good to her and good for her also. He was there by her side when she had cancer, she is a survivor. Our baby sister, Jo or Sylvia as she prefers today, married Gary Ward. Gary was her high school sweetheart also. They have two children, Tamara and Ryan and no grandchildren at this time. Her marriage to Gary ended in divorce also. She later married Tom Yarbro. Patsy and Jo found good men for the second husbands. We all married our high school sweethearts and all of us are in our second marriage, me being widowed, Patsy and Jo from divorce. I believe that the three of us are happy the way life has turned out. I know that that I have been blessed far beyond what I deserve and again I say GOD IS GOOD!

PHOTOGRAPHS

Henry "Buck" King and Nora Gladys Goss

William King (seated) others unknown

Seneca Jones King family
Back row: Eula Colestra, Iley Joel, Hiram Burris
Front row: Seneca Jones, Martin Newell, Henrietta Wheelus King

Mamma Nell, dog Jack and Daddy King

King family

Left to right: Rudolph, R.B., Henry "Buck", Mamma Nell, Daddy King, Bill, Dan, S.J. and Berris. The dog is "Jack"

Sylvia Jo in the car built by Larry.

back: Nora Gladys, Larry
front: Patsy, Sylvia Jo

King Cousins
left to right
Charlotte King, H.B. "Buddy" King, Charlsey King,
Linda Stevens, Annie King
Chi-Chi, Larry King, Patsy King, Linda King,
Shirley Stevens, Kay King

Daddy King and Mamma Nell

Childhood friends: S.J. King holding bow and arrow

Would you like to see your manuscript become a book?

If you are interested in becoming a PublishAmerica author, please submit your manuscript for possible publication to us at:

acquisitions@publishamerica.com

You may also mail in your manuscript to:

**PublishAmerica
PO Box 151
Frederick, MD 21705**

We also offer free graphics for Children's Picture Books!

---

www.publishamerica.com

CPSIA information can be obtained at www.ICGtesting.com
Printed in the USA
BVOW010444051212

307343BV00002B/548/P